The Girl Who Kept Knocking Them Dead

The Girl Who Kept Knocking Them Dead

Hampton Stone

WILDSIDE PRESS

For Berenice and Helena

one

She was pretty, prettier than average. She was young. Estimates put her age at about twenty. Eventually we did get the exact figure. It was twenty-two. She lived alone. There were indications that we'd been expected to think that she died alone, but we never thought that. By the time we came into it, that much was already known, the way the girl had died. It was manual strangulation, and that's a field of endeavor that the do-it-yourself fad is just never going to reach. A girl simply can't put her own two hands around her own lovely throat and choke the life out of herself. It's like wrestling or making love, something that can't be done with less than two people.

Her name was Sydney Bell, except that it wasn't; but we'll come to that later. Let's start with the simple and easy things like who I am and how I got into this business of the girl who kept knocking them dead. That was the way Gibby came to describe it and I'll tell you about Gibby. I can't get far telling you about me without telling you about him.

I am an assistant on the staff of the New York County District Attorney and so is Gibby. You can call me Mac, which is what everybody calls me except in court where things go too formal for that. Since this is anything but a formal report, Mac will do for me. Gibby is Assistant District Attorney Jeremiah X. Gibson, who had once been Patrolman Gibson and later Detective Gibson. That's the way he worked his way through law school. He was on the cops. I didn't know him in those days, but I can tell you he was a good cop. Though I can't speak for the patrolman part of it, on the detective bit nobody knows better. It's in the boy's blood.

Brilliant is the word for Gibby. Sober is the word for me. That's why the DA has set us up as a team. If Gibby has a fault, it's enthusiasm. He'll go out on limbs. I try to see he doesn't go too far out or doesn't get sawed off; but let's face it. He does better than I do. I swear he won't do it to me, but every time it happens. He gets me out on that limb with him. One of these days we'll both be sawed off.

Murder is Gibby's specialty—on the detection end, of course. There aren't many murders happening in our jurisdiction that Gibby doesn't get to work on and, when

4

Gibby's on it, I'm on it with him. The Sydney Bell bit was murder and it happened in New York County. That made it our baby.

It happened in a nice little flat in the West Fifties. One room and bath and kitchenette, but the room was big and bright. It was pleasantly furnished, not spectacularly lush, not austere, but comfortably cheerful. The house had a decent look to it, but in a big city, of course, one never knows. There is nothing anywhere quite so impersonal as one of these apartment buildings. It happens again and again that the people who live in them go on for years without knowing the first thing about their neighbors and it's not until something happens that they even begin to wonder whether the tenant in 5F had been exactly what she seemed to be.

Even then this thing that happens has to be something pretty big. What did happen to the tenant of 5F was quite big enough, of course, since it was murder; but it was evident that it was only when the police started asking questions that any of Sydney Bell's neighbors gave her more than the most passing of thoughts. This one remembered her from meetings in the self-service elevator. Another remembered visitors who came and went. She had many friends, but nobody could describe them closely or tell us anything much about them.

Among the neighbors a rather tart young woman who taught school and lived in 5E, which put her next door to Sydney Bell, came closest to telling us something we could use. Her name was Nora McGuire. Gibby questioned her. It wasn't easy. She went all out to impress us with how broad-minded she was and what a high

5

value she placed on privacy, both her own and that of her neighbors. She didn't want to answer questions. She wanted to mind her own business.

It didn't take Gibby long to break that down. A girl had been murdered in her bed and there was only the apartment wall between that bed and Nora McGuire's place. She could hardly call anything that had come as close as that none of her business. Nora McGuire conceded the point but she argued that she hadn't known that her neighbor was going to be murdered. If she had known, she might have taken a greater interest in her and in the comings and goings of her visitors.

Even without taking any interest, however, she had noticed a few items and, after he'd worked at it awhile, Gibby drew those out of her. She had noticed a woman who had visited Sydney Bell at least twice. She might have seen this woman oftener but of the two occasions she was certain. The reason she was so certain was the fact that this woman owned two mink coats. She had worn a mink of one color on one visit and a mink of quite a different color on a second visit.

"I am that feminine," Nora McGuire said. "I would remember that. I shall probably never even have one mink coat. I could hardly help noticing a woman who had them in assorted colors."

While she was talking to us about mink, a radio was turned on in one of the other apartments in the building. It had come on loud but had quickly been turned down to a civilized volume. Even then, however, it was faintly audible. Gibby waited a bit, listening to the murmur of the radio.

"It's a limited sort of privacy any of us has living in

6

an apartment," he said, after he had given it time to register. "Ever hear anything through the wall?"

"I might have if I had thought to stand with my ear against it or if I'd been equipped with listening devices. Must we go on with this, Mr. Gibson?"

"No ear to the wall, no listening devices. I hear a radio. Don't you?"

"I hear a radio."

She crossed the room, going toward the wall beyond which lay 5F. For a moment I thought she was going to put her ear against the wall, but she didn't. She went to her record player and started some music going. It was Chopin, not notably loud. She walked away from it.

"What's that for?" Gibby asked.

"I don't hear the radio any more," she said. "I like music and when I'm here alone I have it going practically all my waking time. Even when I have visitors there's likely to be music, and if there isn't, it's because I'm that much interested in my guest's talk. Either way I'm not hearing sounds from next door. They're blotted out by the sounds I have right here or possibly I blot them out because I am more interested in these sounds than in those. In any case I don't hear them."

"The volume of that radio when it first came on, you would have heard that."

"I have normal hearing. The point is that there never were any loud sounds from 5F."

Gibby smiled at her. "See," he said. "You can be helpful when you try."

"Is that helpful?"

"It gives us something. We know now that if there

ever was a wild party the other side of that wall or a screaming quarrel, it happened when you weren't home. In other words, she led a quiet life or a stealthy life."

"A quiet life," Miss McGuire said firmly.

"Except that quiet lives don't often end in murder," Gibby said. "But you don't have to worry about that. Let's get back to the people who visited her."

Nora McGuire wasn't quite ready to go back to that.

"I did hear something," she said. "It's not the sort of thing I imagine would interest you, but it was something."

"Everything interests us," Gibby told her. "We know so little about this neighbor of yours that anything at all is an item for us even if it helps only in the smallest possible way toward learning what sort of a person she was."

"I think she had a new job or something was going on the last couple of days that changed her habits," Miss McGuire murmured.

She seemed to be thinking the thing out as she went along.

Gibby cut in on it. "Don't think on it," he said. "The trick is to tell us just what you know, not the conclusions you might draw from it. Conclusions can come later."

"It was this morning," she said, "but this morning was the second time. Yesterday morning was the first."

"You heard something yesterday morning and you heard it again this morning?"

"Yes. Not anything that means anything. It was just her radio. Both mornings when I woke up I could hear it playing the other side of the wall. She didn't have it on loud, not blasting or anything like that. I got up and started my records going and then I didn't hear it any

8

more. It wasn't any louder than the radio you heard from somewhere in the building, but it was on. I did hear it both mornings."

"When you woke? You have a regular waking time?"

"I set my alarm for seven."

"And she was up before seven and playing the radio?"

"Not loud enough to wake me. My alarm woke me and I just heard it over there while I was getting up and before I put my records on."

"You're sure it was a radio you heard in there?"

"Oh, yes. That early morning sort of music and an announcer's voice. One of those singing commercials about detergents."

"The same both mornings?"

She frowned. "Yes," she said. "I'm certain of it, the same singing commercial both mornings. The same announcer's voice. The other music, the bit I heard of it, was different, a different tune."

"And it was radio and not television?"

The question startled her. "Now really," she said. "I couldn't look through the wall and see which it was. That's a silly question. The point I was trying to make is that, for whatever it's worth, she was up and had the thing playing these last two mornings. I've lived here a year and she was in her apartment before I moved in and yesterday was the very first time I heard any sort of sound over there in the morning."

"You have heard it other times of the day though?" Gibby asked.

"I suppose I have. I can't answer with any certainty. I may have heard it dozens of times without ever noticing. I wouldn't notice if I had the records going or if I was busy with anything else. It was just waking to it that way set me listening for the few moments until I was out of bed and started on the day."

"Yes, naturally. I was thinking of last thing at night. Last night and the night before, about what time did you go to bed?"

"Eleven o'clock. Why?"

"That would be another time like first waking in the morning. I should think you would have heard it then if it had been on."

She shook her head. "I hope it doesn't matter," she said, "because I wouldn't have heard it. You see I always put a stack of records on the machine when I'm getting ready for bed, the sort of thing I like to fall asleep to. It goes on playing till I'm asleep and then it plays on till it's through the last record and it turns itself off."

Gibby shrugged it off. "Can't be helped," he said. "You see it does matter because she couldn't have been up and playing it this morning. She had already been dead a good twenty-four hours by this morning."

Nora McGuire gasped and swallowed hard. "But I heard it," she protested.

"I know. That means either that someone was in there playing it or that it was playing when she died and never was turned off till the body was found. You see, if you could have told us that it definitely wasn't playing when you went to bed last night, we could have drawn conclusions from that."

"I'm sorry. I honestly wouldn't know." She thought a moment. "The maid who found her," she said. "She must know whether the thing was playing this afternoon when she went in. If it wasn't, then you definitely know someone was in there and turned it off. It was playing this morning. I can swear to that."

"Good," Gibby told her. "It might be very important. Now, let's get back to her visitors."

She started to pull back. "Now don't think every time she had visitors I saw them," she said. "It was only when I met someone by accident in the elevator or the hall."

"We understand."

"There were men. Possibly four or five times. Once I came in after the theater—it was about a month ago, I think—I met her in the elevator with a man. We rode up together and then she gave him her key. He was opening her door for her when I went into my own place."

"He go in with her?"

"I don't know. I didn't wait to see."

"But you think he might have gone in?"

"Men have brought me home from the theater and I've had them in for a drink. It is done, Mr. Gibson."

"Sure," Gibby murmured. "See the same man more than once?"

"If I did, I didn't notice or I don't remember. None of them wore mink. There was nothing to make me notice."

"But you have the impression of more than one man?"

"Let's put it this way," she said. "If it had been the same man every time, I think I should have noticed. Since I never did notice, I think it was probably different men."

"And since you didn't notice, they must have been pretty ordinary sorts."

"No Hottentots. No turbaned Moslems."

"No Greek gods?" Gibby asked, taking it on her own terms. "No scar-faced lugs, no seven-foot basketball players, no circus midgets?"

"Just men, except . . ."

She caught her lower lip between her teeth and she blushed.

"Except?" Gibby urged.

"Except one time," she said. "Damn, this is going to sound terribly Mrs. Grundy."

"Just let it sound McGuire," Gibby said, keeping it light. "We know you're broad-minded and close-mouthed. Now we're also broad-minded. We don't shock and we don't titillate. We just try to catch people who choke the life out of other people."

I'm not going to go through the direct quotes on it. She kept interrupting herself to hedge it around with explanations of how she came to see and hear it, making it just as clear as could be that she had not been spying, that what she knew was only what she couldn't possibly have helped knowing.

What she did know was something that was a little like the episode she had already given us, the man who brought her neighbor home after the theater and who may or may not have gone in for a drink. This one, however, was different. This time Nora McGuire had again been coming home from the theater. She had met no one in the elevator. On the fifth floor, however, she had seen a man at the door to 5F.

She hadn't even looked at him. She had been trying to find her key in her purse. She had gone to her own door, still looking for the key, and she had only just found it when her neighbor opened the door to 5F. She had heard the man ask for Sydney Bell and she had heard Sydney Bell ask him in. That was all. Her key had turned up by then and she went into her apartment, as the man went into Sydney Bell's.

"I didn't give it a thought," she said. "It was her business, but now with all these questions you're asking, I did remember and I suppose it was a strange time for a man to come visiting her, particularly a man who apparently didn't know her at all."

"You got the impression that she had been expecting this man?"

"Oh, yes. Most certainly."

"This happen recently?"

"No. Months ago. I don't know just when."

That was the whole of it and it was more than we were ever to have from any of the other neighbors. Some of the others, as a matter of fact, were eagerly co-operative, but that was only a matter of attitude. They had nothing to give us apart from their willingness to give.

What we actually had at the beginning of this thing, aside from these tantalizing bits and pieces Gibby did manage to extract from Nora McGuire, was a small collection of quite as fragmentary and quite as tantalizing snippets of physical evidence. We had in the first place the body of Sydney Bell herself. I have already said she was young and pretty. We could to some extent see that from the body, but as Gibby had told the McGuire girl we hadn't seen the body until after she had been more than twenty-four hours dead, and in that length of time an appalling lot of prettiness goes.

Just how much had gone we knew right away because on the table beside her bed she had a framed photograph of herself and, as Gibby put it, that was convenient for us even though a bit oddly narcissistic on her part. It was one of those tinted jobs, all pink and white and golden, with bare shoulders and a froth of filmy stuff just below the shoulders, but you could compare it with the body and, even if you made the reservation that in life she couldn't have been quite so technicolor as that photo, you could say that the nose had been like this and the eyes like that and the mouth like so and the sum total something that would hardly have been hard to look at.

There was only the one other picture in the place. That was also a studio job but rather the better for being in black and white. It also stood on the bedside table. It was the picture of a man or possibly of a boy. Which you would call him might very well depend on the angle your own age might give you on an infantryman who looked as though he had just made Pfc. You know those photographs. This one was at least as much a picture of that single Pfc. stripe on the sleeve and of the combat infantry badge and campaign ribbon over the tunic pocket as it was of the young soldier himself.

He was an earnest looking lad of possibly twenty-one or twenty-two, certainly no more than that. The expression was pompously solemn and a bit stuffed but it was a clean-lined, lean face, with an honest-looking eye and a firm mouth. He might have been a little soft in the jaw department but he wasn't chinless. If there was a really noticeable inadequacy anywhere it was at the top of the head. His hair looked unusually thin for his apparent age.

I remembered him when Nora came around to talking about Sydney Bell's callers, but I couldn't make him fit into that pattern. I had a feeling that he would have to have been older or possibly a sight more dashing to have been one of them. Even before we had talked to Nora, I had been wondering about him.

"A little young for a boy friend," I'd remarked to Gibby.

"Could be an old picture," Gibby said. "A lot of men who don't go for being photographed at all did get the idea they were hot stuff in uniform. They do it then and then they don't do it again. There are battle stars on the campaign ribbon. Those can't be more recent than Korean War which is a little more than yesterday. If they're World War II, this can be a ten-year-old picture or more than that."

I took it the other way. These years Gibby was adding to the age of the kid in the soldier boy picture would have to be subtracted from what was obviously Sydney Bell's approximate age at time of death. I decided it would have to have been Korean War because ten years back or more Sydney would have been much too young to be receiving affectionately inscribed photos from soldiers. She would hardly have been in her teens then and the inscription read: "All my love, Milty."

So there was Milty and there was the body of Sydney Bell. Her cleaning woman, who had a key to the apartment, had come in at her usual time to do the place up and had found the body. This was a twice-a-week cleaning woman and she hadn't been in the day before. It had startled her to find Sydney in bed. That had never happened before and the cleaning woman made it quite clear that she was a person who didn't hold with sleeping past noon and also that in her profession time was money. She had come to clean and she started cleaning. Asleep or not, Sydney Bell was not going to have more than the hour she was paying for.

"I had it figured," the woman said. "I'd start cleaning around her, she'd wake and get up. She was going to have to get up so I could make the bed anyhow and, the way I figured it, she'd be getting up and wanting a shower and all and then how was I going to get to do the bathroom in her hour and all? So I wasn't being careful or anything. I kept bumping the bed like, figuring as how the quicker I woke her up, the better it would be. I bump the bed like that a couple of times and she don't even turn over or stir or nothing and then I begin thinking it's funny. I go over and look at her and right off I see she isn't asleep at all. She's dead and like laid out on the bed with the covers pulled up to her chin. That's when I started yelling."

We knew all there was to know about her yelling. She had done it at the window and it had brought a policeman up to the apartment. He had taken it from there. He hadn't recognized murder right off but he had recognized death and the doctor he had summoned had completed it—death by manual strangulation. In all justice to that cop, there had been a good enough reason for his not seeing it. The body had been dressed in one of those deals that happens as a result of the sleepwear manufacturers going cute.

Remember—it was a couple of years back—all the stores went Victorian or something with red flannel nightgowns, both male and female, red flannel nightcaps, complete with tassel? That was it. Sydney Bell's body was dressed in one of those red flannel nightgowns. Hers was the female type, of course, and it was a fancy one.

16

It had a sort of furry collar on it that buttoned up under the chin. It wasn't fur, but it was white and fluffy, one of those fake furs they make out of synthetics. It covered up every last trace of the marks of strangulation. You see, it wasn't until the doctor started undoing buttons that they showed up at all.

It was seeing that bit in the first report that came through that made Gibby ask the DA if he didn't think this might be just our kind of a case. The DA was non-committal. It could be a difficult one and it could be a cinch, too soon to tell.

"Much too soon," Gibby agreed, "but, as I get the picture, this gal was strangled and her collar was buttoned up afterward. I'd like to ask some questions about that little item."

The DA, who is really great stuff on racket setups and corporation executives who get too smart with their bookkeeping, has never been any sort of a murder man. I don't say there haven't on occasion been DAs who were nothing better than political slobs, but our boy isn't one of those. In his own field he's terrific and he's big enough to know his limitations. Knowing them, he sends the murders Gibby's way.

"If you say so, Gibson," he murmured, "you'd better get up there and ask your questions. Take Mac with you, keep reporting, and work it the usual way."

"Thanks," Gibby said.

"One thing before you take off," the DA asked. "Why couldn't she have been strangled collar and all?"

"Innocent until proved guilty, boss," Gibby said.

"And what does that mean?"

"I always like to assume a man knows his job till something proves it otherwise," Gibby explained. "The doc who's seen the body says manual strangulation. He can't possibly know any more than strangulation unless he has seen marks on the throat that are unmistakably the marks of hands. If anybody took a double handful of throat, furry collar and all, and choked this dame to death without hands slipping off collar to make direct contact with skin of throat, there could be no hand marks on the throat, no marks to say this strangulation is manual strangulation. It could be a garroting, for instance. Now if it had been this thin chiffon stuff, or lace, there would be no question, but a furlike fluff, that's protective padding."

The DA nodded. "You'd better go ask your questions," he said.

Gibby had asked them. He'd begun with the cop. The cop had seen not the first sign of any violence. He had found the room neat, about as neat as a room would be when it was in the process of being cleaned. The bedclothes had been straight and tucked in all around.

"Like it was fresh made or like it was a hospital maybe," the cop said, elaborating the point.

The body had been dressed in the red flannel deal with the furry collar and the collar had been buttoned all the way. He was certain of that. We saw the nightgown and it was evidently of a piece with the neatness of the bedclothes. It didn't even look as though it had been slept in, much less that its wearer had come to a violent death in it.

There was, of course, always the possibility that the maid had done some neating up between yelling for the police and the arrival of the patrolman. Gibby was quick to check her on that and she couldn't have been more emphatic on the point. She hadn't buttoned up any collars and she hadn't touched the bedclothes. She hadn't touched either Miss Bell or the bed except to bump the bed a little in the hope of waking her.

"Look," she said, "my job, it's to clean the apartment. I don't do no undertaker's work."

That's the way the thing had stood when we went to talk to the neighbors. After we'd had the stuff about detergent spiels at seven o'clock two successive mornings, we had a second go at the maid.

"When you came into the apartment this afternoon," Gibby asked, "was the television on?"

"What would she have the television on for and her asleep?" the maid muttered, countering question with question.

"And her dead," Gibby said, tossing it in as though it were only the most minor of corrections.

The maid turned detective. "The way I see it, the poor thing, she was murdered in her sleep," she said. "It comes of young ones like her living alone. I'm sure I don't know what their mammas are thinking of. I never slept even one night away from home, not till I was married, and then it was only away from my folks' home. I was with my husband, God keep him."

"You're positive it wasn't on when you came in?" Gibby tried to nudge her back onto the track.

"What wasn't?"

"The television."

"No. It was like now, turned off."

"Could you have turned it off yourself and then forgotten?" Gibby asked. "It would be playing when you came in and you took no special notice until you realized she was dead. Then, waiting for the police, it would get on your nerves and you would switch it off."

"If it was on when I come in, I would have noticed and switched it off right away. I don't hold with wasting electricity that way. Electricity costs money and you don't go burning it up playing televisions in your sleep. I wouldn't have turned it off when I saw she was dead. I know better than that. A person's dead, you get help. You don't go touching anything. I didn't touch a thing once I seen she was dead and before that only carpet-sweeping the floor a little, but then I didn't know she wasn't just sleeping."

"Very proper," Gibby murmured soothingly. The woman was going just a bit shirty in her protestations of knowing just what was done and what wasn't done. He tried another approach. "You've been cleaning her apartment for some time, haven't you?" he asked.

"Ever since she came to live here and that's going on two years now."

"Good. What was she like?"

"Sweet. She was the sweetest thing. There's never been anyone like her. It breaks my heart, thinking of what that robber done to her."

"Robber?" Gibby asked.

"Robber," the woman said. "What else?"

"You know her place well. You'd know if there was anything missing?"

"I know what's missing, all right," the woman growled.

"Suppose you tell us."

"I'll tell you. I'll tell you, all right. It was all there the last time I cleaned and today it's gone. Every last bit of it gone."

"Every last bit of what?"

"Everything," the woman said, and indignation was

bursting out of her. We seemed to be getting the explosion of something that had been smoldering for some time. "Every last thing she had, it was any good, all her underwear with the nice, black lace on it, all them sheer nylon and lace nightgowns like she was always wearing, all her real good dresses like the evening dresses and the cocktail dresses, even her nice shoes, the high-heeled ones with like diamonds in the heels. Right through all the drawers, right through the whole closet, not even one of them things left, and all them things was mine. She'd promised them to me."

Every tone of the woman's voice was vibrant with growling cello notes of a sense of loss. I was careful not to catch Gibby's eye because I was a cinch to laugh if I did and, if Gibby wanted answers to the questions he was asking, laughing at her wouldn't help.

It was more than a little ludicrous, though. It wasn't that the woman was so old. Fifty perhaps or possibly well up in her forties, but she had gone to flesh. She had gone to quite enough flesh to take her well past even what might be called the stylish-stout dimensions. She was well over into the outsize department, and Sydney Bell's figure had been purely wolf bait. I worked at wiping out of my mind's eye any picture of this babe in underwear with black lace on it eight or ten sizes too small for her, a cocktail or evening dress as small. I looked down at her feet. She was wearing grayish canvas sneakers that bulged over her bunions. I concentrated on imagining those feet in high-heeled shoes with brilliants studding the heels and I got over my impulse to laugh. That wasn't a funny picture. It was pathetic.

"She had promised you her good clothes?" Gibby asked and his face was a mask of the most sober interest.

"Had she been planning something where she wouldn't need them any more?"

I was asking myself what she could have been planning unless it had been suicide and I've already been into that. When it's manual strangulation, it just can't be suicide. Gibby, however, was asking the question, and Gibby doesn't ask questions just to hear the sound of his own voice. In a situation like this, more than ever, I have yet to hear him ask a completely idle question. I tried to figure him and I came up with a beaut. Could it have been a suicide pact?

Suicide pacts aren't too common, but they do happen and a large proportion of them never get done all the way. He kills her, by agreement, and he is to kill himself immediately afterward. He means to do it, of course, but his nerve runs out. We've had them like that. Also it wouldn't even have to be like that. He killed her and he went off somewhere else to dispose of himself. He would have to have used some other method on himself in any event. He could have gone down to the river and in. He could have thrown himself under a subway train or a truck. He could just have gone home to his own place and shot himself or hanged himself. There were all sorts of possibilities.

I was doing all this thinking but it wasn't taking me any time to speak of. The thought hit me and the possibilities just whizzed through my mind. Immediately they whizzed out again. The woman was answering and her answer took care of the suicide angle quite to my satisfaction.

"No," she said. "Not like that. She was always giving me her nice stuff, real nice stuff, and it was still brand-new. When she would get through with something, it

22

was not like some they give you things is only fit to wear cleaning house or like that. It's had every last bit of good worn out of it. Miss Bell, she wasn't like that. She always had to have the latest, whatever it was. She'd go shopping and she'd buy herself a dress, say. She'd bring it home and hang it in the closet. She wasn't going to crowd her stuff up it should get crushed just hanging. She'd take out some dress she had from before and she wore it maybe ten times, maybe not even that, and she'd give it to me. It was like that all the time."

"I see," Gibby said. "You felt that all her nice things she would be passing on to you one day."

"She promised me. She always said when she was through with a thing, nobody got it but me. My Gloria— Gloria, she's my daughter—my Gloria, she's so much like Miss Bell they could even be sisters. She's a size twelve and a perfect figure. Something it fits Miss Bell, it's a dream on Gloria. The things they look better even on Gloria than they ever looked on Miss Bell, because my Gloria, she's got more style. Miss Bell, she'd bring home a new evening dress, real gorgeous, and she'd tell me like it's now September I should tell Gloria about it because Gloria can figure on it for the Firemen's Ball New Year's Eve. That was just the way Miss Bell talked because my Gloria, she don't go with firemen or like that. Who wants a fireman? They're never home when you need them. When you've got him, where is he? He's playing pinochle over to the firehouse. Then he falls off a ladder or something and you're still young and what have you got? A pension?"

Gibby had to nudge her back on the track again, because once she got going on her daughter Gloria, her talk began running very thin on items that were at all germane to any preoccupations of ours. Slicing Gloria out of the harangue, I can reduce it considerably. Sydney Bell was constantly buying clothes. What she bought was of the glamorous persuasion and it was costly. She never wore anything for more than perhaps four months and often for less time than that and the stuff was still in prime condition when she would give it to her cleaning woman for daughter Gloria.

This procedure, furthermore, covered everything she wore. It wasn't only the dresses. The pursuit of the *dernier cri* was equally relentless in all departments—undergarments, shoes, sleepwear, everything.

"Even nylons sometimes," the woman said. "She has drawers full of nylons, some of them she never even wore, and then they come out with something new like it's a new shade and the stockings so thin all you can see is their seams. You can't tell one shade from another once they're on, but Miss Bell, she has to have the new shade or the shell soles or the heels high and pointy in back or whatever it is, and she gives me all the nylons out of her drawer, some she ain't never even had on at all."

"And everything's gone?" Gibby asked. "Even her nylons?"

"No," the woman said grudgingly. "Not the nylons. They're still there and there's one set of underwear—old lady stuff like maybe I'd buy for myself except it's her size and in the closet nothing but her suits and her coat. They're in there and two dresses, real plain, but nothing really nice, not even a nightgown except that flannel thing she was wearing and the good Lord only knows how she came to have that. She never had nothing like that long as I've known her or that one set of underwear in the empty drawer."

24

She went on about how she didn't even know whether Gloria would want to wear any of the things that were left, except the suits and the coat and the nylons. They were nice. She was bitterly contemptuous of the underwear and the red flannel nightgown.

"Flannel," she said, and her voice dripped contempt. "Since when is she wearing flannel to bed? Red, yes, but it's sheer red nylon with lace set in it here. That was her style."

She indicated the location of *here* by patting her own too ample middle, but we got the idea. Sydney Bell, however sweet, had been the flaming seductress. We had what amounted to a stitch by stitch description of the sheer red nylon nightgowns with the lace set into them. The woman wanted to know what a girl who was wont to cover her fair white body with loveliness of that ilk would be doing with only one set of underwear in her drawer, and that old-ladyish. She also wanted to know what could make a girl who was accustomed to red nylon and lace let herself be caught dead in unglamorous flannel.

"You had a good look around," Gibby said. "When did you manage that?"

The woman took the question in her stride. She was too much outraged over all the treasure that had slipped out of her Gloria's grasp to have a thought for anything else.

"I seen she was dead," she said, "and I yelled. Then I was up there with her and waiting for the cop to come. What was I to do? Stand there looking at her that way, dead and all? I thought of all her lovely things and I thought I'd look at them for the couple of minutes while the cop was coming up. I opened the closet and I come near fainting. Then I looked in her drawers. I seen enough by the time that cop rang the bell."

We took her into the apartment. The body had long since been removed and the police lab boys were in there. They were giving the place the works—fingerprints, dust samples, the full scientific detection routine we have done on any murder scene. While we had her in there, the boys fingerprinted her. She didn't like that much but Gibby's explanation satisfied her. She had been in there cleaning. She had touched things. She had herself volunteered that she had opened the closet and various drawers. As fingerprints turned up in the place, the freshest ones were likely to be hers.

"That don't mean I done anything," she protested. "I done just like I told you."

Gibby reassured her, explaining that we could hardly eliminate from the picture such obviously innocent fingerprints as hers unless we had hers for identification. She was a bit restive about having them taken but she submitted with not too much fuss.

With her guidance we went through the drawers and the closet. It was quite as she had said—no low-cut gorgeousness, no nylon transparencies, no black lace seductions. There was only the sparsest of sparse wardrobes. Not a spare nightdress, only one solitary set of underthings, and nothing anywhere that Nora McGuire next door might not have primly worn for her schoolteaching.

"Even her laundry," the outraged cleaning woman said. "She'd drop things in the hamper I should rinse them out for her when I come in. Even them things, her dirty things, they've been swiped, too."

We covered the whole place. The bottle of Scotch was

gone. Nothing left in that department but the soda. Gibby wondered about papers. There were no letters or papers of any kind and the cleaning woman dismissed those quickly. There never had been any. She had seen Miss Bell when she would go down for her mail. She would read a letter and throw it away. She wasn't one to keep stuff, the woman said.

We did find her purse. It was in one of her drawers along with a handsome assortment of other purses and a collection of smart-looking gloves. This one purse was evidently the one she had carried last. It contained the usual cosmetic items but it also contained money, $250 in bills plus a couple of dollars in silver. The cleaning woman took that discovery as the crowning outrage. This had been the meanest kind of burglary, she felt. Nothing had been taken except the things that would ordinarily have passed on to her for her Gloria, nothing except the Scotch and the cigarettes. Gloria was a good girl. She had never tasted a drop in her life. She didn't smoke either.

We made another discovery and that also outraged Gloria's mamma. In the drawer with that one set of demure underthings we found a prayer book and a couple of tracts. The tracts were those Jehovah's Witnesses sell on street corners.

"Them," the cleaning woman sneered. "None of them was ever around here before. Who wants them?"

The last of it was we had to get her out of the apartment. Gloria could use the suits and the coat and the nylons and the bags and the gloves and, since they would have been hers anyhow when Miss Bell would have been through with them and nobody could say she wasn't through with them now, Gloria's mamma came down with the idea that she might just as well pack up anything her Gloria could use and take it right off with her.

Gibby had to explain about the possibility of a next of kin. He did the best anyone could with it, but Gloria's mamma wasn't convinced.

The things had been promised to her. It was injustice. That's what it was.

two

Her cries of injustice were by no means the whole of it. She was also a theorist. She wasn't content with simply yelling burglary. She insisted that we look for a burglar who was also a ghoul. Miss Bell was dead. She had known Miss Bell well. Miss Bell would never have been caught dead in a flannel nightgown. Therefore it followed inevitably that Miss Bell had not been wearing that red flannel when she had died. The burglar had stopped at nothing in collecting the loot. He had even stripped off the poor girl's body one of those glamorous red nylon-and-lace jobs and substituted for it that detestable flannel.

We had Nora McGuire in from next door. The high-value-on-privacy girl could go on indefinitely making all her nicely turned points to the effect that she had never had the slightest interest in her neighbor's habits, but she had already confessed to us that she was enough a woman to have taken some considerable notice of her neighbor's clothes. We asked Nora to look over the things in the drawers and the closet. Nora was appalled. She remembered a pink satin evening coat. She remembered several dazzling dresses. She was by no means as letter perfect in the late Sydney Bell's wardrobe as was Gloria's mamma, but she remembered enough. None of the party clothes she had been seeing on her neighbor's back were now to be found in her neighbor's apartment.

She had, of course, no knowledge of the lingerie or the nightdresses, but she did give it as her opinion that the items in that department, as described by Gloria's mamma, would have been the sort of thing she would have expected. Sydney Bell had not been the flannel nightgown type. They were agreed on that.

They left us with something to think about. I turned to Gibby.

"What now?" I asked. "Do we go hunting the ghoulish burglar?"

"That," Gibby said. "Or else we concentrate on the religious tracts. I don't know that they aren't worse."

I didn't quite follow him there but he sketched enough of it in and I was able to take it from there to fill out the whole picture. Party girl murdered. Every last physical trace of her party-girl life removed. Girl left looking like the complete Miss Prim in death. Prayer book and religious tracts among her things. Start reconstructing from that and see where you come out.

It's all too easy. Sydney Bell has been leading the gay life. She goes out partying. Men call on her, even at strange hours. She has fun. Then she meets a man and this man is different. He's a serious type who talks religion at her. Would Sydney Bell have had any time for a type like that? One never knows. The wilder forms of religiosity do have a way of turning up in extraordinarily virile and ardent people at times.

You must understand that this isn't religion we're talking about. It's insanity, the kind of insanity that comes of guilt feelings gone out of hand, the sense of sin run amok. This type sets out to save the girl's soul. He calls it that in his twisted thinking and he believes it. She goes for him. She's saved. She makes the clean sweep of all her fripperies, all the trappings of that sinful life she used to lead. Next stop the Kingdom of Heaven, but the poor girl hadn't dreamed it could be that quick. This crazy type she's fallen for does one of those quick twists you have to look for in people who have set up housekeeping in a fantasy world. Abruptly the whole picture turns itself inside out for him. He hasn't saved her soul at all. She has led him into corruption instead. He rears up out of her sinful bed, puts his hands around her fair, white throat and chokes the life out of her. Then he buttons her up neatly to the chin. It's in character. His sense of propriety has been satisfied, and he goes his crazy way.

In any murder case, as soon as the surrounding circumstances begin to take on a peculiar look, somebody is bound to come up with the easy out, a mad killer. The thought is, of course, that, having a collection of evidence which you cannot make add up into any rational pattern, you can just stop trying, tick it off as the work of a madman, and call it one that cannot be expected to make sense. Actually it is never quite that simple. The mad killing is not without pattern. It may follow a mad pattern but within its own crazy frame it will be rational enough.

The possibility of a madman in the Sydney Bell killing was not one of those things that popped into our heads because we were feeling baffled and defeated. The evidence had begun to form and it was giving sharp indication that it might be shaping in that special direction. It wasn't the easy out. It was a conclusion to which we might very possibly be forced, however reluctantly, because when they are like that they can be awfully tough.

Meanwhile, of course, Gibby was quite right. It was no good trying to forget the possibility of the madly righteous loon but it was also no good settling for anything that definite, at least until we had done all the available digging along all the lines that presented themselves.

We had just gone into a huddle with the lab boys to see whether they might have something that could be a lead for us, when the cleaning woman came pounding back in a fever of excitement. She knew where all Miss Bell's lovely things had gone. She could take us there and show us.

"It's only around the corner," she said. "Secondhand clothes it is and never a thing in the window that isn't from five years ago and nobody, they're anybody, is wearing it any more until just now I went past and I seen it right away. One of Miss Bell's beautiful red night-gowns—nylon and lace and all sheer like she had made

34

special for her all the time—one of them is in the window and inside I can see hanging the pink coat and the new evening dress with the harem skirt."

We let her show us the way. It was, as she said, just around the corner, and the shop looked as unprepossessing as she had described it. A sign in the window said they bought and sold used clothing and the stuff on display could hardly have looked more used. It was a crowded window except for a space in the center of it. That space was empty.

Gloria's mamma gasped. She pointed at the empty space.

"It was there only a minute ago," she said. "Right there."

We could see through the window into the shop. A rather frowzy woman who unmistakably had the second-hand look was in there with a man. She was holding up for his inspection something that was so red and so filmily transparent that it looked like a tongue of flame. It had lace on it and the lace appeared to be in just that area that Gloria's mamma had described to us as *here.*

The cleaning woman dug Gibby in the ribs and pointed. Gibby nodded. He made no move. He just watched through the window. We made quite an audience at that window. So much so, that I began to feel a bit crowded. There were the three of us but there were two men as well and they all but had their noses pressed to the windowpane. I glanced at them and dismissed them as not worth a second look. I may have wondered a bit at their being interested in this window, but I also dismissed that.

They could see that red nightgown the woman was showing to the man inside. No man who is a man can look at one of those things without immediately dreaming up a picture that would put some dame into it and it wouldn't be just any dame either. It would be something luscious, but necessarily. Tossing off the pair who were outside looking in as a couple of idle dreamers, I concentrated on that more enterprising character inside who appeared to be on the road toward implementing his dream.

That was one big hunk of man. He had a very yellow look, but it was the look of the outdoors type who happens to be having a spot of ill health. You know how a really dark suntan looks when the healthy, red blood isn't coursing under it. This lad had been out in the sun plenty, but under the bronzing he was carrying an unhealthy pallor.

His clothes didn't help. He was wearing a reddish brown suit and a reddish brown shirt and a yellow tie, colors calculated to make a sick man look sicker. The shop's show window had been modernized with a surrounding trim of mirror glass and I noticed that this gent's color scheme seemed to be repeated in the glass. I turned my head to have a look at what was reflecting in such splendid combinations of brown and yellow.

It was an enormous convertible, parked at the curb, a very special-looking job of bronze paint and yellow leather upholstery. It was an easy guess that the convertible belonged to the man in the shop. He was dressed to match it. Another car, far less spectacular, was double-parked just outside the big bronze and yellow job.

I turned back to the show window and a new detail caught my eye. The mirror glass reflected the convertible's license plate. It was a Connecticut license—one of those that is all letters and no numerals—and in the glass it read JERK. That seemed too comic and I turned back for another look at the car. Of course, the plate read KREJ.

Meanwhile inside the shop the man, whom I was now in my own mind calling Krej spelled backwards, dug in his pocket and brought out a couple of bills which he gave the woman. She put the luscious red nightgown in a bag for him. The two men who had been watching with us moved. They didn't move far, only to the shop door. There they waited; and when the big boy came out with his package, they fell in on either side of him.

"Hi," they said.

"Hi," he answered in a husky whisper. "What brings you over here?"

He started toward his car and then he turned back to his two friends, scowling. He had seen how the car double-parked outside him had him boxed in.

One of the men laughed and they both came in beside him again and very close.

"We've been chasing you, stupid," the one who was laughing told him. "Mae's got a party going and she asked me to bring you. Seeing as how we've been watching you buy that red thing, you can't pretend to us you won't be in the mood for the Mae bit tonight."

The big fellow didn't relax the scowl. "If you move so I can get out," he said, "I'll see you over at Mae's later." It was still the husky whisper. He sounded as though he had lost his voice, was trying to get it back, and wasn't making it.

They moved over as far as the convertible where they held a whispered huddle. After a moment, the huddle at the curb broke up. More exactly it moved around the Cadillac to the car that was double-parked outside it. They went in that same formation they had held in crossing to the curb. The big man was in the middle. The two others were beside him, one on either side, and they walked close. The one who had done all the laughing and talking got in the car and big boy got in beside him. He was still clutching his parcel in his massive mitt. With his free hand he was passing over a ring with keys on it to the remaining man. That third one hadn't gotten into the car.

Gibby made a quick dash out into the street. I went with him. We met the one with the key ring just as he was turning toward the Cadillac. It was close quarters there between the parked cars and Gibby kept going almost as though the man wasn't there. Gibby rammed right into him and pushed him backwards. When Gibby came to a standstill, he had the man backed tight against the car and there was no question that he was holding him there.

"What the hell?" the man said, clawing ineffectually at Gibby's arm.

Gibby ignored him and talked past him to the big boy with the yellow face.

"Anything we can do for you, mister?" he asked. "It looks as though you're in trouble."

The big boy went some shades yellower. "Trouble?" he repeated, stupidly echoing Gibby's word.

"These two ganging up on you?" Gibby asked.

The vocal one of the pair had had his foot on the starter. Now he took it off and laughed again.

"Us gang up on him?" he said. "He could whip the two of us with one hand tied behind his back."

"How about taking him with both hands tied behind his back?" Gibby asked. "You could handle him then, couldn't you? Especially with a gun."

38

The man stopped laughing. "Look, mister," he growled, "maybe you're drunk or something. Maybe you'll go away now and bother someone else."

"Your buddy here hasn't the gun," Gibby said. "He's clean."

As though he were demonstrating the fact on the man he had crowded against the side of the car, Gibby slapped him smartly in all the standard, concealed-weapons places.

"You're not drunk," the man behind the wheel said. "I can see that. What's with you anyway? You take it in the arm?"

"District Attorney's Office," Gibby said and brought out his credentials.

None of the three even bothered to look at them. I've never seen people more easily convinced.

The man who had been doing the talking climbed out from behind the wheel.

He was talking as he came. "I suppose I could start yelling," he said. "I have a hunch there's all kinds of rights I have in a thing like this, but what the hell, you want to feel me up, mister, go ahead. Have your fun. Only look out you don't tickle. People tickle me, I get the hiccups and when I get them I go on forever."

He came around into that narrow space between the cars and he put his arms up at his sides. Gibby ran him over.

I don't know whether I had been expecting a gun or just hoping for one. This was one of those limbs Gibby goes out on and when you're out that far, brother, look out. You had better be right. This character did have all kinds of rights and Gibby was walking over every last one of them. He didn't find a gun. He didn't yield an inch. He wasn't letting them see it was bothering him. I hoped vaguely that I was managing to play it as dead-pan. I had a feeling anyone could have seen how much it was bothering me.

"No gun," Gibby said. "What's the setup?"

"Setup? We're friends. We spot his car in traffic. You'll give us that. It's no trouble to spot. We want him on a party we're having, so we pick him up. I know we're double-parked, but it's only for a minute and since when is the DA's office handing out the traffic tickets?"

Gibby looked to the big boy. He was still hanging on to his package and he hadn't found his voice. He had to try twice before he made even the husky whisper come.

"They're my friends," he said. "We're going to be late for the party. The dames, they'll get sore we keep them waiting."

"Okay," Gibby said, stepping back out of it. "Have fun."

"We can go now?" It was the man who hadn't bothered to yell for his rights who did the speaking.

Gibby nodded.

"Thanks," the man murmured with only the smallest edge of sarcasm on it. He slid back behind the wheel and put his foot on the starter again. "See you," he said to the man he was leaving with us.

With a wave of his hand, he pulled away. He was carrying New York plates. Gibby wrote down the number.

The man who had the Cadillac keys shook them and made them jingle. "Brother," he said, breathing a sigh of relief. "You nearly tore that one."

Gibby looked at him coldly. "Feel like talking?" he asked.

40

"Only to ask how come you didn't smell the liquor on his breath," the man said. "How far do you think he can drive with all that liquor in him before he's pinched or even has an accident? This isn't the first time we've talked him out from behind the wheel. You don't know, but I do. He can be stubborn. Stubborn, and how. He's all right now. I'll put the Caddy in the garage for him and I don't turn up with the keys till he's slept it off. What did you think we were doing? Kidnaping the little fellow?"

"I didn't like his looking so yellow," Gibby said, "and getting much yellower the minute he saw you."

"It's an old story with him. He isn't pretty when he's drinking."

The man got into the Cadillac. He was all affability now. He even asked if he couldn't drop us off somewhere.

We weren't going anywhere just then. I shook myself to get some of the creep out of my flesh. "It's a good thing they were that nice about it," I said. "There's the time you really went overboard."

He talked right past my words. "They didn't look like male nurses," he said. "Even working in pairs, male nurses should be bigger."

"They said they were his friends and so did he," I said. "You went over both of them and no guns. What's wrong with believing them?"

"They didn't look like friends," Gibby insisted. "When two men close in on a third that way and crowd him that close, they're letting him feel that they've got guns on him and he hasn't got a chance."

I didn't even attempt to argue that the thing hadn't looked that way. Just on the way the men had closed in on either side of Yellowface, on the way they had moved with him to the curb, on the way they had taken him to the car, it could have been a Police Academy demonstration of how a pair of gangsters might pull off a snatch out in the public street. I stuck with the point I could make. Appearances had been deceptive. It hadn't been at all as it had looked. Gibby had checked and neither of the men had been carrying a gun.

Ramming his hand into his pocket, Gibby shouldered in tight against me. A lightning-fast jab caught me in the side just at that soft place between the rib cage and the hip bone. I have seen men who've been shot and the bullet's point of entry was just there. It's a bad place. They get it there and they don't survive it. Furthermore they don't die quickly or easily.

"Am I holding a gun on you?" Gibby asked.

I laughed at him. "That was your thumb, kid," I said. "You aren't carrying a gun."

"Suppose you didn't know I'm not carrying a gun, would you be all that sure then?"

"Completely sure. I know you. If you had a gun on you, you wouldn't be playing games with it."

"Suppose that hadn't been your old pal, Gibson. Suppose it had been one of those friends of the Jerk spelled backwards, how certain would you have been then?"

"I would have been in a cold sweat."

"And the big guy was in just that."

I'd known he would be building to that and I was ready for him or I thought I was.

"Not at the end there," I said. "Not after you had checked on the both of them and found no guns. He couldn't have been afraid of a thumb in his gut. He's too big a guy for that."

"If he believed me," Gibby muttered.

"Why wouldn't he believe you? Would you go looking for concealed weapons, find them, and then change your mind?"

"That's what keeps me thinking there was something funny about all that," Gibby said. "The two who had every reason to make an ugly fuss over my stepping in and crowding them like that were really docile about it. Since when do we get to throw our weight around that way and all we have to say is DA's office and we get all that respect for it? They were too good-natured and they hardly looked at my credentials. I could have done it just as well on my driver's license. I could have been Joe Doak, practical joker, and done it on a traveling salesman's business card. And the boy they were pushing around, he didn't look at all. Couldn't he have been worrying about some really fancy trick, all four of us out to take him together?"

I was about to take the line of least resistance by reminding him that we already had a murder we were working on, but by that time Gloria's mamma had tired of staring balefully through the shop window. She came over to the curb and joined us there.

Gibby took her by the arm and we went into the shop. He asked the woman in there whether she had any more red nightgowns like the one she had just sold. The woman went into a quick song and dance about how very special those nightgowns were. It was the build-up for asking such a price as wouldn't often be named in a place like that.

I think Gibby, for a while at least, would have played it along as though we were merely shopping, but Gloria's mamma gave the show away. There wasn't any help for that. She began going through the place and pulling out one thing after another.

"See," she kept saying. "This is mine and that's mine and that over there is mine."

The woman who ran the place was, of course, lightning-quick to go on guard.

"What is this?" she asked. "What do you want?"

We showed our credentials and Gibby started asking questions. It wasn't the first time we had talked with a fence and we recognized all the answers the woman had ready. She had bought these fine things over a period of several months. She had bought them from various people, none of them regular patrons of her shop. She didn't think she would recognize the people if she were to see them again. None of the items Gloria's mamma was claiming had she bought within the last few days.

That was her story and she couldn't be shaken from it. Even when Gibby told her she was covering for a killer, she wouldn't budge. Gibby didn't waste much time on that. He went into action. He called the apartment house and had one of the cops over there ask Nora Mc-Guire to come around the corner and join us. She came, and although she couldn't speak for lingerie, she did back Gloria's mamma up on the pink evening coat and a flock of dresses.

Gibby took it from there. He impounded the identified items and gave the shopkeeper a receipt for them. Then he turned them over to one of the Homicide detectives. It was going to be this man's job to trace them back to the places where they had been bought. It was a cinch that some of the stuff at least would be pinned down as not even having been manufactured at the dates when

44

this woman said she had bought them. She would break down eventually, but it was going to take time, a lot of time.

One of the police lab chaps came down to talk to us. He waited restlessly while we finished what we had to do in the secondhand-clothes store. At that point Gibby thanked Gloria's mamma and Nora McGuire and sent them on their way. Nora went with good grace. Gloria's mamma went off repeating her cries of injustice. We went out to the street with the lab cop. We left the dame in the store to utter her own cries of injustice, but those were no more than normal expectancy.

That cop was the fingerprint man and he had the dope on prints. He looked about as agog as those boys ever get. Those lab cops, after all, are the scientists of the police department and for the most part they work very hard at their air of scientific detachment. This boy's detachment had come detached.

"We've got a little honey in this one, Mr. Gibson," he said.

Gibby wasn't going to be easily impressed. "All prints wiped clean?" he asked.

"Yes and no," said the cop.

Gibby gave him a hard look. "When did you start talking like a girl on the porch swing?"

The cop grinned. "Yes, the whole place was wiped clean of prints," he said. "But no, the place wasn't clean of prints."

"Anything we can use?" Gibby was still not impressed.

It happens often enough, more often than not in fact. Fingerprint evidence has been so well publicized. Everybody knows about it. Almost anyone bent on crime these days knows enough to wear gloves or wipe clean any surface he has touched. You get it all the time that a place has been carefully wiped up to remove all prints, but one or two surfaces will have been forgotten. Practically anyone will think of doing it. Many aren't nearly methodical enough to do a complete job of it. This cop, in his experience, should have seen dozens like that. It seemed strange that this one should excite him so much.

He shrugged. "I don't know how you'll use it," he said, "but maybe you can make something of the fact that the dame lived there and in the whole place we can't bring up even a fragment of a print that will fit with hers."

Gibby's interest quickened. "All wiped away?" he asked.

"Even in the places they mostly don't think of like the toilet seat," the cop answered.

"But you did get prints?" Gibby asked. He was eager now.

"Two people's prints. We have an easy make on one of the people, that cleaning woman you've been working on."

"Where did you turn hers up?"

"Knobs on the front door, inside and out. Knob of the closet door and panel of the closet door. Soiled clothes hamper in the bathroom. Front of every drawer in the place. Footboard of the bed."

Gibby was scowling with concentration, making an evident mental check of each location the cop mentioned.

"And another person?" he asked.

"Clear prints well spread over the apartment. Small fingers, probably a woman's. Not in our files and we've

46

put them through to the FBI for a check with their central file."

"Too soon to have anything on that yet," Gibby muttered. "You say well spread over the apartment. What specific locations?"

The cop consulted a list he was carrying. He read it off for us and it did sound as though this unknown had covered the place completely, touching just about everything in sight. These prints had been turned up on the closet door, on several empty hangers found in the closet, on all drawer fronts, on both headboard and footboard of the bed, on all the cupboards in the kitchenette, on the toilet seat in the bathroom, on the taps of the bathroom washstand, on a can of cleansing powder in the bathroom, and on the porcelain of the bathroom washstand. He spoke specially of this last set.

"The ones on the washstand," he said, "they're the doozies, Mr. Gibson. Both hands, left and right, and all ten fingers. It's like they'd been done for the file, perfect and complete. I've been doing this for a long time, and I've never picked up another set like them."

We went up to the apartment with him and he took us into the bathroom and showed us the exact position on the washstand where he had been able to bring out these phenomenal prints. The four fingers of each hand had turned up on the sides and the thumbs had turned up on top. Gibby smiled grimly.

"No wonder they're so good," he said. "She had her whole weight behind them."

The cop shrugged. "Craziest one I've ever seen," he said. "Don't forget this was after wiping the place clean."

"I'm not forgetting," Gibby said.

We were moving out of the bathroom when the bell rang. The cop knew all about the bells. He had been working in there most of the afternoon and there had been plenty of coming and going, what with all the police and the Medical Examiner's men.

"That's the downstairs bell," he said. "One of our fellows coming back that'll be."

He put his finger on a button that would release the lock on the downstairs door. He held it there for a few moments.

"Expect any of your men back here now?" Gibby asked.

"We'll be keeping a man on here tonight anyhow—" the cop began.

"Just in case some of her friends should turn up," Gibby said, finishing it for him. "Someone has turned up. It can be one of our boys. It could be someone for her. Let's not assume anything."

The cop flushed. He was a specialist and evidently a bit rusty on the general run of police routine, but he was still a cop. He made an apologetic gesture. Nobody said anything. We were waiting. In the quiet I could hear Nora McGuire's record player next door. It was coming through pleasantly as just the most discreet murmur of music. The sudden, sharp shrilling of the upstairs doorbell made me jump a bit.

Gibby moved to the door and opened it. A young man with thin hair stood on the doormat. He was all big grin and dancing eyes. He saw us and the grin faded and some of the gaiety went out of his eyes. He went into a flutter of apologetic gestures.

48

"Oh, I'm sorry," he said. "I must have the wrong apartment."

"Come in," Gibby said. "You have the right apartment."

I thought he was just riding a hunch. In fact, it did strike me that this could very possibly belong to Nora McGuire next door. He looked the type who might join her for a high old time with Frédéric Chopin on the gramophone.

Then he came in and the light fell full on his face. Just for verification, I took a quick glance at the picture on the bedside table. He was looking some years older and he wasn't in uniform, but there was no mistaking him. Even without the combat infantry medal or the Pfc. stripe, this was Milty, the only man in the life of the late Sydney Bell on whom we had anything more than Nora McGuire's vague descriptions.

At that moment he stuck his hand out and introduced himself. "I'm Milt Bannerman," he said. "You know, Ellie's brother."

Since nobody had taken his hand he now used it to gesture toward his picture where it still sat on the table.

"Yes," Gibby said. "We recognized you from the picture."

"Both the girls out?" Milty asked. "Serves me right, I suppose, for trying to surprise them. They weren't expecting me till tonight. I found I could get an earlier train."

"You were expecting to find your sister here with Miss Bell?" Gibby asked.

For just a split second Milt Bannerman looked confused. Then he laughed.

"Of course," he said. "You know her as Sydney Bell.
That's Ellie. That's my sister."

He made that gesture toward the table again but this
time it was at the dead girl's picture.

"Then what other girl were you expecting to find here
with her?" Gibby asked.

Milty started to speak. The beginning of a syllable
did come past his lips, something that sounded like
"Jo—" but he bit off sharply and with a wary eye
on the three of us he started edging toward the door.
The cop wasn't so much the fingerprint lab specialist
that he didn't quietly move with Bannerman, putting
himself in the doorway behind him.

"Hey, what is this?" Bannerman asked. "Who are
you anyway and where are the girls?"

Gibby introduced himself and while he was at it, he
also introduced me and the officer who stood in the doorway.

Bannerman's wary look took on a sharper edge. His
eyes narrowed and there was that almost imperceptible
change all over him under the decent blue suit. Muscles
were settling themselves. Mentally he was pinning the
combat infantryman's badge back on his chest.

"You'll have some sort of identification," he said. "I
don't just have to take your word for it."

Gibby showed him his identification. I brought mine
out and the officer stood with his in his hand. It couldn't
have been more different from the previous time we
had shown them. If Gibby had been questioning the
readiness of those characters out in the street to take
us on our own say-so, he could have no complaint of
Milton Bannerman's thoroughness.

He didn't just look at our credentials. He made a study of them. He examined all three in turn and he was so long over each that he could have been memorizing them unless he was a very slow study. I didn't think he was memorizing them. I thought he was playing for time.

three

Gibby was giving him all the time he wanted, but it couldn't last forever. Eventually Bannerman handed everything back and stood waiting.

"Well?" Gibby said, trying to prod him a bit.

He didn't take it. "Okay," he came back. "I'm still asking the question. Where are the girls? Something's happened. That's obvious. How long are you going to play around with me? Tell me and get it over with. They're all right, aren't they? They've got to be all right."

"We only know of one girl," Gibby told him, "the

girl who lived in this apartment and called herself Sydney Bell. You call her Ellie. Ellie Bannerman?"

"That was her right name. Eleanor. Eleanor Bannerman. Where is she? What's happened to her?"

"When did you see her last, Mr. Bannerman?"

He didn't even consider answering that one. By now he was showing every evidence of being thoroughly frightened and thoroughly angry.

"Now, look," he said. "I'm through answering questions. I'm asking them from here on out. If Ellie's in any kind of trouble, I don't know the first thing about it and I'm the only one who has any right to know. I'm her brother. I'm the only one the kid's got in the world and I want to see her. I also want to know what's happened to Joanie and I'm not waiting either."

"Who's Joanie, Mr. Bannerman?"

"Never mind who's Joanie. Now, look, mister. I'm going to have some quick answers or else."

He had his hands in his pockets and the pockets were bulking big. He had balled his hands up into fists. He looked as though he might be just about ready to bring them out and start swinging.

"Suppose you cool down, Mr. Bannerman," Gibby said. "It's not going to help anything if we start blowing our tops."

Bannerman blew his top. "I have no intention of cooling down," he shouted. "I come here expecting to find my sister and my fiancée. They're not here. You won't tell me where they are and you start throwing all these funny questions at me. Now I don't know what you think you're doing, but I do know that I don't have to answer anybody's questions and I've got every right in the world to be asking a lot of my own. I'm asking them and I'm going to have the answers and quick, or else."

"Or else what, Mr. Bannerman?" Gibby asked, slipping the question quietly into the echoes of Bannerman's shouting.

Bannerman brought his hands out of his pockets. He looked at his fists for a moment and then slowly, reluctantly, opened them out till his hands were spread in front of him in a gesture of helplessness.

"Or else," he said softly, "I'll have to find me a lawyer. I don't know where I stand here, but I do know there's something wrong with all this . . ." He paused searching for the words. After a moment he came up with them. "There's something awfully wrong with all this highhanded nonsense," he said.

It was one of those situations. You may think Gibby was just playing the man, but there isn't any easy way of handling it. Of course, you have to come out with the bad news sooner or later, but if you can get as much information as possible before you break it, it's likely to be a big help. Once the word's been spoken, once a relative has heard the word *death*, you can be a long time before you'll get another question asked and a longer time before you'll get one answered. Gibby hadn't gotten much but he decided it was no use trying any longer. Milton Bannerman had dug in his heels. We had to give him some answers.

"Your fiancée," Gibby began. "We don't know anything about her. . . ."

Bannerman broke in on him. "Don't give me that, brother," he said. "She's been living right here with Ellie. She's been here a whole week. Don't tell me you don't know anything about her."

"We haven't been here a whole week, Mr. Bannerman," Gibby said patiently. "We came in only today and as far as we know there's been only the one girl living here, the girl who called herself Sydney Bell."

"Yes, that's Ellie. Sydney Bell, that's the name she uses on her job." He stopped short. Something had gone a bit wrong with his breathing. He swallowed hard and spoke again. "You said 'called herself Sydney Bell,' " he muttered. "What do you mean 'called herself'?"

"Sydney Bell is dead," Gibby said gently. "The woman who cleaned for her came in early this afternoon and found her dead."

He stood quite still for a moment, stunned. Then he shook himself, just as a dog does coming out of water.

"Is this some kind of a gag or something?" he asked. "It isn't funny. It isn't a bit funny."

"It isn't funny," Gibby said. "She was killed. Murdered, Mr. Bannerman."

"Ellie? You're crazy. Who'd kill Ellie? What would anyone want to kill a kid like her for?"

"We're going to have to find that out."

Bannerman charged toward Gibby. He grabbed up a big fistful of the front of Gibby's coat.

"Joanie," he said. "Was Joanie here? What's happened to Joanie?"

Gibby made no move to push him off.

"I know this is rough," he said. "But you must see that we're not giving you a hard time. It's the facts about your sister that are rough. There's nothing we can do about those right now, but there may be something we can do about your fiancée."

Bannerman shook Gibby a little. "You leave Joanie alone," he stormed. "You hear me? You leave her alone."

Gibby backed him toward a chair and pushed him down into it.

"Now look," he said. "I'm laying it on the line. We don't know the first thing about Joanie. We hadn't the first idea that she was supposed to be here. Just try to remember we're on your side. You want to find her and we want to help you find her. We can't even get started unless we know her name. We'll try to find her for you, but give us her name. Give us a description. Answer some questions, man."

Bannerman spoke but the words were coming through tight, stiff lips. We had to strain to hear them.

"She came here last week," he said. "She wanted to shop and Ellie invited her to come stay with her. Ellie was helping Joanie with her shopping, Ellie knowing the stores here and all. I was supposed to be coming in tonight and the way we had it fixed I'd go to the hotel and wash up and come right over here. They were going to be here waiting for me. I got an earlier train and I thought I'd surprise them. Now this."

"Your fiancée?" Gibby asked. "Does she know anyone else in New York? Anyone she could have gone to?"

He shook his head. "Nobody here in New York," he said. "Nobody at all in the East except some cousins she's got in Boston. She was . . ." He broke off and beat his fists against his forehead.

"Come on," Gibby urged. "Come on. Don't stop to think."

Bannerman sighed. "No," he said. "That's no good. She wouldn't be up there now, expecting me here tonight."

He explained that Joanie had planned to go up to

Boston for a couple of days during her week in New York. She had promised to visit these cousins of hers but he felt certain that she would have done that earlier. She couldn't possibly have planned it so that she wouldn't be in town for his arrival.

"Do you know the name of these cousins?" Gibby asked.

"Hale. Mrs. Stephen Hale. They live on something I think it's called Fenway. Is there a street called Fenway up in Boston?"

"I hope there is," Gibby said. "We'll try it. Is that Joanie's second name, Hale?"

"No. Mrs. Hale's her cousin. It's Loomis—Joan Loomis."

I picked up the phone and dialed long distance. I got Boston Information and had them dig for the number.

"There is a Fenway," I said. "They're looking up Hales."

"Thanks," Bannerman murmured. He turned back to Gibby. "Tell me about Ellie," he said. "How did it happen? You're sure she's dead. Not just missing or anything like that? Dead?"

"She was strangled," Gibby told him. "Killed. It's murder. I'm going to have to ask you to identify the body, since you're the next of kin."

It occurred to me that it had hardly been established that he was the next of kin. All we had was his own word for it that he was the dead girl's brother. I put the thought aside. It didn't matter too much at that point. If he was lying to us, confronting him with the body could do no harm and there might be a lot of use in it.

There wasn't any recoil from the idea of seeing the body.

"I want to see her, poor kid," he said. "I want to take her home to bury her, of course. Ellie, murdered. How does a thing like that happen to a little kid like Ellie?"

Information came up with the number.

"They're ringing the Hales," I said.

Gibby dropped his hand on Bannerman's shoulder. "Do you suppose you could talk to them?" he asked. "There's no use telling them anything and throwing a scare into them if we don't have to. Just ask if she's up there or been up there. She could be on a train coming down right now, not expecting you till later tonight."

Bannerman nodded. He got out of the chair, came over and took the phone from my hand. He was shaking.

After a couple of moments he spoke into the phone.

"Mrs. Hale?" he said. "Gert? . . . You don't know me. I'm Milton Bannerman."

That produced one of those joyous cries at the other end. There's a certain pitch the voice of an excited woman can reach at the telephone that makes it carry like nobody's business. It's only certain types of voices that will do it and this was one of those voices. Bannerman must have caught the zing of it against his eardrum because involuntarily he moved the receiver about an inch away from his ear and held it there. It was coming over like a public address system. We could all hear it.

"Joanie's Milton Bannerman? We've been hearing all about you. You have to come up and see us. We're dying to meet you, but Joanie's already told you that. Is she with you now?"

"No, she isn't, Gert. As a matter of fact that's why I called. You see we've got crossed wires or something down here. I got into New York a little early and went around to my sister's thinking I'd surprise the girls. Well, they're not here, not either of them, and I just thought maybe Joanie was with you and would be coming down on a train that would get her in just before I was supposed to turn up."

"Oh, no, Milton. She was up here. She told you she would be coming up for a couple of days. Well, she did. We had a lovely visit and she left last night. It was later than I liked but there are these friends I did so want her to meet and I couldn't get them over before last evening and Joanie said it wasn't as though she hadn't already been in New York and didn't know the way. She was sure she could get a cab at Grand Central and go right over to your sister's even though it was going to be all of three in the morning when she got in. I wanted her to stay and take an early train this morning, but she said you were coming today and she didn't want to take any chances on not being there when you arrived."

Bannerman had been white when he first took up the phone. Now he had turned the color of wet ashes.

"You say her train got in at three o'clock this morning?" he moaned.

"Oh, dear," Mrs. Hale laughed. "Don't sound so tragic. The porters in Grand Central are the sweetest things. They're like somebody's grandfather, really. And cab drivers are so reliable, especially the ones that work out of the railway stations. You just wait. They're out shopping. After all, they aren't expecting you this early. Now when are you bringing Joanie back to visit us?"

He mumbled something and got off the wire. He turned to us and began to repeat it.

"We could hear," Gibby said.

Bannerman swayed on his feet. He shut his eyes tight and breathed hard for a moment, getting a grip on himself.

"Oh, God," he groaned. "Ellie and now Joanie, too. Three o'clock this morning."

"Hold it," Gibby said. "It's bad enough as it is. Don't build it. Does Miss Loomis know the train you were supposed to be coming in on?"

"Yes, but they weren't going to go to meet me. Ellie said you can miss people so easy in stations. She said for me to come over here. They'd be here."

"All right. Miss Loomis got here at three in the morning. Your sister had been dead for quite a while by then. She rang the bell and got no answer. She's gone to a hotel and she'll be back here in time to be here for when you were expected or else she'll go to meet the train she's expecting you on. We'll cover both. We'll have someone waiting here in case she comes. We'll go with you to meet the train. One way or the other we'll find her."

It sounded all right to me but it wasn't my sister who had been strangled and it wasn't my fiancée who was missing. Bannerman took more convincing than that.

"You don't know Joanie," he said. "I do. She wouldn't come turning up here at three in the morning to ring bells. It would have to be that she had a key and could come in without disturbing Ellie. She would have a key, staying here with Ellie, Ellie would certainly have given her one so she could come and go. She came in here and Ellie was dead but there was someone here. It's the both of them. I know it's the both of them."

The point wasn't too badly taken. I couldn't see any such complete certainty of it as he was proclaiming, but it certainly had to rate as a disquieting possibility. Gibby, however, made a good stab at pulling him together.

"If we want to start imagining things," he said, "we can imagine it any way at all. There's nothing to go on. For one thing, how certain are you that she was staying here with your sister at all? Just look around. There's only the one bed. It's a double bed, but there's only the one. If she stayed here, they shared the bed. There's nothing else like a sofa or anything that could be made up into a bed. If you're going to argue that she had to have a key because she would be too considerate to ring bells at three in the morning, can't you argue on exactly the same basis that she wouldn't come here at all at three in the morning when it would mean coming into this one room, getting into the one bed? Wouldn't that be just as disturbing as ringing the bell?"

"I don't know. Gosh, I don't know. When Ellie said she should come and stay here, I thought sure Ellie had an extra bed. I don't know what to think about anything now."

It was an opening for Gibby. He suggested that Bannerman try not to think at all. There was still a great deal we were going to have to know. We were going to have to ask many questions. If he would try to keep his mind on that, it would help him with the waiting.

"Also," Gibby said, "you'll be helping us and the

more you give us to go on the easier it's going to be for us to help you. Let's start with Joan Loomis. Do you have a picture of her on you?"

He had one and he fished it out of his billfold for us. It was a bathing-suit picture but don't get ideas. It wasn't any bikini. It wasn't even one of those halter and bare midriff deals. It was a cover-up sort of bathing suit and by that I don't mean one of the elasticized jobs that covers a gal but close like an extra skin. It had a skirt and it had a top with fairly broad straps going over the shoulders. If it wasn't the sort of thing Grandma wore in the nineties, it was quite the sort of thing that Grandma might pick out as a decent sort of suit for Granddaughter to wear today. Legs it showed about to the knees. Arms it showed completely. Neck and shoulders it showed a lot less than your stenographer is likely to show at her typewriter any day.

All the same it was a cute suit and a cute girl inside it. The legs were very nice indeed and the figure plenty good enough so you knew that it wasn't for any cosmetic reasons that she wasn't showing more of it. I couldn't tell about hair because there was a bathing cap but the face was nice. Beach pictures being what they are, you couldn't see too much, but I had the idea that Joan Loomis was by no means the lovely thing that Sydney Bell had been but that she would be quite pretty enough in a wholesome, country-girl fashion.

In the description department Bannerman did all right. Height five foot five. Weight 130 pounds. Light brown hair. Fair complexion. Blue eyes. He said her hair was long and she wore it up in one of these knobs at the back of her head. When it came to what she might be wearing he couldn't give us nearly so much. He knew what she had been wearing when he had seen her off to New York. It was a dark gray suit and a pink blouse with a little round white collar that came outside over the collar of her coat.

"She was buying clothes here," he said. "I don't know whether she'll be wearing something she brought from home or something she's bought. Anyhow it's likely to have one of those little round white collars she wears outside. She likes those. She wears them on mostly everything."

I thought I knew what he meant and I thought it sounded something like a school uniform.

"How old is she?" Gibby asked.

It's a routine question. I didn't know whether the schoolgirlish note had struck him or not.

"Twenty-one," Bannerman answered. "Just a year younger than Ellie."

Gibby called the description in. Missing persons could start routine on it in any case. He didn't relax, though. He came right back at the questioning. I have never known a session of this sort to have more of an appearance of going well. Bannerman seemed to be in a mild state of shock, as well he might have been; but, if anything, that appeared to have loosened him up a bit, released some inhibitions he might otherwise have exhibited.

Gibby suggested that we might go out and get him a drink and he was a little prim about that.

"No, thanks," he said. "I don't drink."

The real impact of it was in the tone he used. That tone didn't leave anything unsaid. Here was a boy who had convictions on the subject. He was horrified by the suggestion that he might even have wanted a drink but it was a situation he had faced up to before he had made the journey into the big city. He had known the sort of place New York was. He had known that people did drink there. He had made up his mind, however, to stick to his guns. No when-in-Rome-do-as-the-Romans-do for him, but he would be polite about it. He would say nothing. He would just be firm in his refusal.

It was all there. I could even guess where he had learned it. That would have come in the army. He would be out on pass with his buddies. The other boys would be tying one on or at least stopping for a couple of beers. I could just see this one going around to the USO for a coke.

Gibby acted as though he had missed the "I don't drink" part of it and caught nothing of the tone which made it so clear that in this young man's way of thinking nobody else should drink either.

"There's nothing up here," Gibby said, "but we don't have to stay right here."

Bannerman gave him an indulgent little sad-eyed smile.

"Of course, there wouldn't be anything up here," he said. "This was Ellie's place."

Gibby fished his cigarettes out of his pocket and offered Bannerman a smoke.

"Thank you, no," Bannerman said.

The fingerprint man went to the kitchenette and came back with a saucer.

"Not an ash tray anywhere in the place," he said. "I've been using this."

The three of us lit cigarettes and used the saucer. Bannerman was wearing that little sad-eyed smile again. He was being real big, forgiving us for having made the mistake of thinking his sister might have had an ash tray around the place.

Then Gibby was back to working at him with the questions and he answered readily, as though it might have been some sort of relief for him to talk, particularly a relief to turn backward to areas where he felt he knew all the answers, where there were no terrible uncertainties to clutch at his heart.

There had been only the two of them, his sister Ellie and himself, ever since he had been fifteen and she ten. Their parents had been killed in a bus accident and they had had no other relatives. There had been insurance, not much of it but enough to carry them along for two years while he finished high school and kept them going with after-school and vacation jobs. He had wanted to go on to college but that was out. He had left school at seventeen and taken on the full-time job of supporting himself and his twelve-year-old sister.

He was modest in his telling of it, but the picture emerged. It was a picture of a hard-working youngster who had taken on a man's job and not done badly with it. He had earned their way, had kept kid sister in school, and had been both father and mother to her. He had a feeling of accomplishment and it came through the cover of his modesty. It was evident that not the least of his pride was that he had been able to guide his sister through those difficult years from ten to seventeen and to keep her from the pitfalls of temptation.

She had just finished high school and she had her first job, typist-stenographer in a real estate office, when the deferments on his army service ran out.

"I didn't get called up when I was eighteen like other people," he explained. "I had to support Ellie and they deferred me for that, but when Ellie was out of school and she had a job, they couldn't defer me any more. I had to go then. I didn't feel good about it—not that I wanted to dodge serving or anything like that—but Ellie was only seventeen and nobody to look after her, nobody even to tell her about things. The night before I left, I had to tell her myself. You know, about men and babies and all that Mom would have taken care of."

He didn't labor it. In fact, it seemed to me that he was happy enough to touch on it lightly and sheer away from the thought of the worries he had had for her when she had been only seventeen.

The way he told it, he had certainly been a level-headed kid. He had foreseen this moment when he would have to go, and so far as he had been able to manage it, he had prepared for it. He had put by all the savings he could and he was able to leave his sister so that with her earnings, the allotment out of his army pay, and a monthly pittance he sent her out of these savings, she would be having no financial difficulties. Then the Korean trouble had come and he had known he would be shipping overseas. At that point he had sent her all that remained of his savings along with careful instructions for banking it and drawing on it only as she needed it.

He had shipped and there had been that unavoidable space of time during which no letters could reach him. The first letter he had had in Korea had been a shocker. Ellie had rented their house, given up her job, and moved to New York.

"She wasn't eighteen yet and she'd never been anywhere but River Forks all her life and alone in New York," he said. "I thought I'd go crazy."

"River Forks?" Gibby asked. "Where's that?"

"Ohio. River Forks, Ohio. That's our home. It was bad enough leaving her alone that way in River Forks but we'd lived there all our lives. People knew us. We knew people. She wasn't among strangers. The man she worked for, for instance, Frank Hamilton, he'd been a friend of Pop's. He'd known her from a baby. He was like an uncle to us, or something. See what I mean?"

"What made her come to New York?"

"A girl she had known at high school had been in a beauty contest and had been Miss Ohio. This girl had gone to New York and was working as a model. She had invited Ellie to spend her vacation in New York. More than that she had urged her to pack and come. Modeling was wonderful and she was sure Ellie could get a job and even if she couldn't, she could certainly get a job as a typist-stenographer and in a job like that she would be making three times what she made in River Forks.

"That's what sold Ellie," Bannerman said. "She wrote me all about it, a real grown-up letter. It didn't make sense for her to stay in River Forks working for so little and using up my savings when I could use them after I got back home. We owned the house free and clear. Pop had left it to us that way and there was this housing shortage and she was getting a wonderful rent for it. So with that and the money she could make in New York she wouldn't have to touch any of my savings and she didn't think she would even have to use any of my allotment money. She was going to try to save that up for me too. She had it all figured out just as though she was some fifty-year-old banker or something."

"And she wasn't quite eighteen," Gibby said.

Not quite eighteen. He repeated it after Gibby and

there was the little sad-eyed smile again. He had worried himself half-crazy about her but the letters had kept coming regularly, at least as regularly as letters did come to combat units in Korea. She had stayed with the beauty contest winner for a couple of weeks and had found a stenographer's job right away. After the first two weeks she had gotten herself a room at the YWCA. Then a couple of months later she had found a little apartment for herself.

"Not this one," he said. "It was some place called Queens."

"Yes," Gibby said. "Probably cost a lot less than anything over here."

Bannerman looked at the one room with its kitchenette and bathroom appendages.

"This can't cost much," he said. "There's little enough of it."

Gibby had no intention of letting the thing channel off into a discussion of New York rentals.

"The friend that got her to come to New York," he said. "Do you know her name?"

"Williams," Bannerman answered. "Grace Williams. That isn't her name now. She married somebody. It was just about the time Ellie got that first apartment. I don't know his name. Anyhow she married him. He was here in the navy, I think. He shipped to the West Coast and she followed him out there. Ellie wrote me all about it."

"I thought if we could find some of the people who knew her here in New York," Gibby said, "they could help us."

"She had a lot of friends," Bannerman said.

"Any you know?"

"No. I've never been here before, but from her letters

I could understand she had a lot of friends. Ellie would. People always liked Ellie. She was so pretty and sweet. You just looked at her and you could see what a nice girl she was."

He had still been in Korea when she had begun sending him money. She had given up the typing and she was working as a model. There was far more money in modeling and she was doing wonderfully. She didn't even need the money that came in every month from the house out in River Forks and she was banking all the allotment money for him. He had always wanted to go to college and it had only been because of her that he hadn't gone. Now he would have his chance. When he got back he could go on the GI Bill and it wouldn't even be hard going because he'd find quite a lot of savings she was piling up for him and if he needed more, she would always be able to help him. Meanwhile she didn't want him going without things out there. She wanted him to have everything all the other boys had. She'd be sending him money from time to time and any time he needed any, he was to just write to her. She could send more.

"Modeling," Gibby said. "Didn't that worry you? You were in the army. You were seeing pin-ups and calendars."

Bannerman crimsoned. For a moment he looked as though he were going to fly into a rage and wade into Gibby, but he quickly took a fresh hold on himself and then it was the sad smile again. This time it was definitely a pitying smile.

"You never knew Ellie," he said. "We'd been through all that when she first came to New York. I'd written and told her I didn't like the idea of New York and I didn't like the idea of her being with anyone who worked as a model. I knew Ellie wouldn't do anything like that but after all what did Ellie know? The way I saw it this Grace Williams was probably doing just that, posing for those calendar pictures and Ellie not having the first idea of anything like that. I felt I had to explain it to her and I did."

Little sister had answered that letter and her answer had been reassuring. In the first place, it had demonstrated to him that time hadn't been standing still while he had been away. Little sister knew all that there was to be known about modeling. There were the models he had in mind. She knew about them, but no nice girl would do that sort of work. Her friend Grace had marvelous hair and that was all anyone ever photographed of Grace, her hair. She posed for shampoo ads and home permanent ads and hair tint ads. It was always hair. Ellie had sent him a sheaf of magazine clippings and there hadn't been one in the lot that would have brought even the faintest whistle from even the most lupine of his buddies. It had all been Grace's crowning glory.

"Of course," he said, his face freezing a bit with disapproval, "it was all different colors in all the different ads, but I realized that would be part of the job. Still when Ellie wrote me that she was modeling herself I was mighty glad it was hands and not hair. I wouldn't have liked it if Ellie had to dye her hair different colors all the time, especially some of those colors like strawberry or that very white blonde."

"Ellie was just hands?" Gibby asked.

"Just hands. She sent me a flock of clippings of the ads. Gloves, nail polish, rings, cuticle remover, stuff like that. Sometimes it wasn't anything that had to do with hands really except that they used hands, like a perfume ad where the picture was just Ellie's hands holding up a crystal ball. The perfume was called Oriental Magic."

He wasn't saying that he hadn't worried. She was still alone in the big city. As time went on, however, and Ellie continued writing and everything seemed to be going splendidly, he had grown to believe that little sister could really take care of herself and he had worried less. Her move to Manhattan had been a good example. She had explained about Queens being quite far away from things and how she had a long walk to either the subway or the bus through quiet and lonely streets. She had been most particular to make him understand that quiet in New York was not like quiet at home in River Forks. New York was a city of strangers and some of these strangers were sinister. It was better to live in a part of town where there would always be lots of people around, especially for a young girl alone.

The first New York apartment had come while he was still in Korea. Since then there had been a couple of further moves but always in Manhattan. Each time she had explained that the neighborhood had gone down a bit and, being a girl alone, she felt it was best that she should live in only the most respectable neighborhoods.

"It sounded wonderful," he said. "She was being so careful and all. I suppose I forgot that in a town like this you can be as careful as careful and still it mightn't be enough, but I can't understand it. I'll never understand it."

Gibby nudged him back to the track of his narrative. The Korean War was a long time over and he had told us he had never been in New York before.

He explained that. It had been his first idea that he

would ask for his discharge at a camp somewhere near New York so he could see Ellie as soon as he came home, but he had applied for college admission back in River Forks. He told us about the college. It was one of those little denominational instititions that are so numerous out there. The timing worked out badly. The army was going to be turning him loose just in time to start school and coming to New York would have meant losing a whole semester. He had already delayed this higher education of his for many years but he had been ready to delay it again. He had been that concerned about Ellie.

It had been little sister again who had been the practical one. She was hungry for a sight of him and for River Forks and home. She could take the time. She had told him to get his discharge near home and she had gone to River Forks to be there to meet him. She had done more than that. She had arranged with the people who were renting the house so that they let him have his old room. It had been a fine arrangement. He'd had room and board with a fine family and right in his own home and it had just come off the rent they were paying for the house.

So that had been it. She had come home to River Forks, and New York hadn't changed her at all. She was as pretty and as sweet and as obviously a nice girl as she had always been. She had, of course, grown up. She knew how to handle money and she was so smart and practical that she made him feel like the child. He had stopped worrying about Ellie and had buckled down to the job of getting his degree.

She had wanted to help him with money but he had insisted on standing on his own feet. It hadn't been hard even though he had made her take half the rent money on the house every month because it was half hers. He had done all right what with the GI Bill and a part-time job and all the money she had saved for him out of his army pay. It had been fine. Vacations he had always had a job and Ellie had come home to River Forks on visits a couple of times a year. There had been no reason for him to take the time off from school or work and to spend the money on coming to New York.

The past June he had been graduated and he had a teaching job coming up right there at the old school. He had already started on his Master's in summer school and he had had a summer job, and there was Joanie. They were to be married just before the fall semester opened and they were going to live in his room at the old house. Ellie had wanted him to take the whole house and let her help him for the year or so before he would be earning enough with his teaching really to swing it, but he had refused that.

"We were still arguing about it," he said sadly. "We'd reached the place where she said anyhow she wouldn't take her half of the rent money any more. She was giving us her half of the house for a wedding present. I hadn't agreed to take it. It was too much, but that was one of the things I was going to do while I was here, really find out how she was fixed for money, make sure she was all right. She was going to go back to River Forks with Joanie and me for the wedding. We had it all planned."

And that was his whole story. Gibby dug hard for more but he got nothing. He very much wanted some sort of a lead to who her associates in New York might have been—friends, business acquaintances. Bannerman, aside from being confident that she had had many friends, insisted that he knew no names, had no clues. He didn't even know what modeling agency she had worked with. For that matter he didn't even know what a modeling agency was.

"Men friends?" Gibby asked. "Marriage plans? Anything like that? She must have confided in you."

"Ellie," Bannerman said, "Ellie always told me everything. She never had any secrets from me. She said it was crazy the way some girls were in a hurry to marry and took anyone who came along, boys with all sorts of vices and everything. She said she was waiting for Mr. Right to come along. She knew he would find her some day."

"I suppose she couldn't have known that Mr. Wrong would find her first," Gibby murmured sympathetically.

If Gibby had stuck a pin into him he couldn't have brought on a more startled reflex than he drew from Bannerman with those words. The man's eyes widened and his mouth dropped open.

He gasped. "You think it could have been a man?" he exploded the question at Gibby. "I mean someone she knew, someone she had visiting her?"

"It looks very much like it," Gibby said.

"A burglar," Bannerman said. He was babbling now. "Some kind of maniac."

"She was in bed," Gibby told him. "She was strangled, possibly even in her sleep."

Bannerman shuddered but, when he spoke, he sounded almost a little relieved. "Then it was a burglar," he said stoutly. "Or some lunatic who got in here. Ellie wouldn't have any man in here and she in bed. Come to think of it, she wouldn't have had any men visiting her here anyhow, not living this way in one room with the bed right here in the one room she had. I tell you she knew about things. She wouldn't entertain a man in a room with a bed in it."

"I wonder," Gibby began. The look on Bannerman's face made it all too clear that he wasn't in a mood to brook even a bit of wondering on any such theme. Gibby made a fresh start. "I wonder," he said, "if she mightn't have been married." That wasn't what he was wondering at all but if he had come any closer at that point, it was obvious that Bannerman would have exploded in such a hysteria of outrage that we couldn't have hoped to have anything coherent out of the man ever again.

"Without telling me?" There was quite enough outrage in Bannerman's voice at even that suggestion.

"She could have been keeping it for a surprise," Gibby said.

Bannerman looked at him. He was evidently wondering whether Gibby had gone quite insane or if this would be an example of the sort of horribly sinful thinking that was current in New York.

"How could she have been married?" he asked scornfully. "She invited Joanie to stay here with her. Joanie was here with her till she went to Boston. You can see there isn't another room. There isn't even another bed."

"There sure isn't," Gibby agreed, but he left it at that.

We took Bannerman out of there. We had the car parked out in the street and I waited with Bannerman in the car while Gibby went to a phone booth to get through to the Medical Examiner. That last bit was obviously on Bannerman's mind. He asked me whether in New York girls, nice girls, entertained men in their apartments alone. I told him they did.

"Aren't they afraid of what people will think?" he asked.

"I suppose some are," I said. "In a house like this one for instance, people pay not the slightest attention to what their neighbors are doing."

"But what about the risk? A girl might make a mistake. The wrong sort of man."

"That's another side of living in one of these apartments," I said. "You're alone and you're not alone. Scream and there are a million neighbors to come running."

I put that out on a venture, to see how he would react.

He shuddered. "A burglar," he said. "A burglar, who killed Ellie in her sleep. Ellie never got to scream."

Gibby came back to the car and he was looking most thoughtful.

One of the lab boys came out of the house and came to the car. He had a little something for us. They had been into the incinerator and had found some fused glass.

"Could be nothing," he said. "People throw empty bottles down those things all the time but it's all that's recognizable except for the usual unburned bits of quite ordinary garbage."

"Anything that could have been clothing among those bits?" Gibby asked.

"Nothing. We've checked most particularly."

We ran Bannerman down to the morgue and we left him in the waiting room while we went in for a preliminary look at the corpse. I couldn't quite see the point of that since we had already seen Eleanor Bannerman's remains and I couldn't see that it made any difference that at the time we had still been calling her Sydney Bell.

As soon as we were away from Bannerman, however, Gibby explained. The ME had told him that he had finished with her. There were the visceral samples that were going through laboratory analysis and we were going to have to wait for those analyses before we would know whether she had been drugged or anything like that; but the rest of the post-mortem examination had been done and the results were quite as indicated, death by manual strangulation.

"There's one thing I wanted to look at before we took him in," Gibby said.

"What thing?" I asked.

"Do you remember her fingernails?"

I did remember. The fingernails had gone with the red flannel nightgown and those other simplicities the cleaning woman had so emphatically insisted were uncharacteristic. They had been without polish and clipped very short. When we had seen the body they had seemed to me quite in keeping. The fact that they had been by no means in keeping with the picture we'd had of the dead girl from her maid and her neighbor had not come to my mind. There could no question that they were in keeping with Eleanor Bannerman's brother's picture of her. I said as much.

Gibby gave me a look of blank incredulity. "How do they fit with his story of what she's been doing?" he asked. "Modeling hands. Do you think she was doing some stop-biting-your-nails ads?"

I had been too much absorbed in the nice-girl side of brother Milton's story. I had completely missed out on the staggering discrepancy. I suggested that Gibby kick me from slab to slab.

The attendant pulled her out for us.

"This whole fingernail angle has been nagging at me," Gibby said. "I was wondering about it from the first, and when brother said she had been modeling hands, it got much too peculiar. I asked the ME if he had looked at them and he had. He can't be certain but he says it isn't a bad bet that possibly they were clipped after she was dead."

We examined the hands and Gibby pointed out to me a couple of fingers the ME had mentioned specifically. It was the doc's opinion that on those fingers the nails were clipped so very close that it would have been an agonizingly painful operation unless the girl had already been dead or at least unconscious.

I thought of the young man we had left waiting outside. He didn't smoke. He didn't drink. Calendar art horrified him. He put great emphasis on a girl's being a nice girl. Before he had even come on the scene the thought of religion and righteousness gone astray had inevitably suggested itself. Abruptly it was something far stronger than a suggestion. His sister had deceived him all these years. He had come to New York and made the horrible discovery. In his righteous wrath he had killed her and had erased all the symbols of her sinful life. Could this erasing of symbols have included that savage job of nail clipping?

I had done my thinking aloud and Gibby concurred with it at least in part.

"One possibility," he said. "There is also another. Suppose the girl struggled. Women in the process of being strangled have a way of clawing and scratching. It's been publicized almost as much as fingerprint evidence. You know, the microscopic fragments of skin and hair found under the victim's fingernails indicate that her assailant was a man fifty years of age, four foot tall, weighing five hundred pounds and with a strawberry mark just above his right nostril."

The attendant, who had been listening wide-eyed, interrupted at this point.

"Nobody who is four foot tall could weigh five hundred pounds," he said.

"The height and weight," Gibby said, carrying it off completely dead-pan, "are only estimates. They can be off an inch or two or a pound or two either way."

That took care of the attendant. He subsided into mumbling softly to himself and Gibby turned back to me.

"Yes," I said. "Of course. You wipe up everything to erase fingerprints and you clip the fingernails so close that there can't be any microscopic bits of you left under them. Nothing there for the microscopic bits to be under."

We went back outside and brought Bannerman in. He hadn't been a soldier for nothing. It's no good saying he took it like a man because there are plenty of men—and it's no reflection on their manhood—who when they have to make one of those morgue identifications, can't take it at all. He made the identification and he said a short prayer over her. He asked whether he couldn't get started on the arrangements for her funeral. He would have liked to have her out of the morgue as quickly as possible. Gibby promised to expedite that for him.

We expected that would be all, but Bannerman came up with a surprise.

"Joanie," he said in a small and sickeningly tentative voice. "If something's happened to Joanie and she hasn't been identified, she might be here right now, wouldn't she?"

Gibby admitted that it was a possibility.

Bannerman squared his shoulders and stiffened into grim, military bearing. He could have been posing for a recruiting poster.

"If there are any girls who haven't been identified," he said firmly, "I had better see them."

"Perhaps you had better," Gibby said dryly.

We took him out with us while we checked. There was only one unidentified body of a young woman and we went back in to have a look at that. It was a redhead with freckles who had been hit by a truck in a traffic accident. She wasn't Bannerman's Joanie, not by a good forty pounds of fatty tissue and a flock of other details.

"That leaves us hope," Gibby told Bannerman. "It leaves us a lot of hope."

"Yes," Bannerman said.

That is, he tried to say it but it was no great success. We had to hurry him off to a place where he could be sick, which he was, spectacularly and protractedly. When he was through we knew it wasn't any good offering him the drink he so obviously needed. It was equally not any good expecting him to carry on as white and shaken as he was.

We just had to give him a bit of time to rest and pull himself together by whatever means of his own he might have. We did that and his means seemed to be prayer. Watching him, I had every expectation that it was going to work, but actually it wasn't tested out. Gibby used the time to get on the phone. He called in to check on how well Missing Persons might be doing on the hunt for Joan Loomis. They were doing all right.

The boys didn't actually have Joan Loomis on hand for us but they did have an encouraging lead toward a Joan Loomis who answered the description Bannerman had given us. As we already knew, she wasn't in the morgue. A check of the hospitals had produced nothing. The next step, however, a check of hotels, had been helpful. A Joan Loomis, registered from River Forks, Ohio, had been turned up at the President Polk. Miss Loomis was not in her room and she had not responded to paging, but there was one of the bellhops who remembered her. He had taken her up to her room at 9:30 that morning when she had checked in, and it was evident that he had studied the young woman with that appraising eye which a bellhop will inevitably turn on the ten-cent tipper.

The description he had given the cops who had talked to him had included the fact that she had tipped him only a dime. As they relayed it to Gibby, he had described her as a young chick with the makings of a dish except that she was already a young old maid. He remembered a gray suit, a gray hat, and a white collar like one his sister used to wear when she had been going to some convent school.

The boys had asked the desk and they got the same check-in time, 9:30 that morning. The clerk further remembered that Miss Loomis had come down from her room not more than fifteen minutes after checking in and had left her key at the desk. She had been out most of the day but had returned at the end of the afternoon well loaded down with parcels. Another bellhop had tried to take them from her but she had stubbornly insisted on carrying them herself. It was the opinion of the President Polk staff that she had been saving a second dime tip. This time she had spent perhaps a half hour in her room and then had gone out again, again leaving her key at the desk. The boys from Missing Persons had come along only a few minutes later. They were now settled in there waiting for her to return.

Gibby asked them to keep on it. He was ready to hang up when the headquarters operator cut in and said they had something else for us. Gibby had turned in earlier the registration numbers on the two cars that had been parked outside the secondhand-clothes store. The Connecticut registration that was Jerk spelled backwards belonged to a man named Jellicoe, Kirk Reginald Emmenthal Jellicoe. They were rushing this news to Gibby because they now had something else on a Kirk Reginald Emmenthal Jellicoe. A patrolman had picked up a beaten-up drunk on Madison Avenue and the man had given the officer that sesquipedalian name. The officer had taken the man down to Bellevue for treatment. They thought we might want to know since Gibby had put through the query on the car registration. Gibby said we were happy to know, particularly happy since we were at the morgue and, the morgue being an adjunct of Bellevue Hospital, it could hardly have been handier. He went over to Bannerman.

"Looks like we've located Joanie," he said.

Bannerman leaped to his feet. "Where is she?" he asked.

"At the moment I don't know. At 9:30 this morning she checked in to a hotel. She was all right then. She went out and she was gone all day but she came in for half an hour not very long ago and then went out again.

Anyhow we have that much. She was on her feet and evidently in perfectly good shape late this afternoon. No reason to expect she won't be the same way when we find her."

Bannerman looked as though he wanted to believe it. He wanted to be happy but he was afraid to believe anything.

"How do you know it's she?" he asked.

"She's registered as Joan Loomis of River Forks, Ohio," Gibby told him. "She also answers the description you gave us."

"I'd better go to the hotel and wait for her," Bannerman said, starting for the door.

Gibby caught his arm and held him. "Rather do that than meet your train?" Gibby asked him.

Bannerman looked at his watch. "Yes," he said. "The station first. She must be there right now waiting for my train."

"We'll run you up there," Gibby said. "There's still time. We'll take off as soon as we've gone around the corner to the hospital and had one of the doctors give you something."

Bannerman had lost all interest in medical assistance. He had even forgotten about prayer.

"I don't need anything now," he said. "I'm fine now with this news of Joanie. That was better than any medicine."

He wasn't just saying it. He looked it. He looked, in fact, every inch the eager bridegroom except for one thing he did have to bother him and that was some inner necessity to look less happy than he seemed to be feeling, since such a look would be suitable for a young man whose little sister had so recently been done to death by manual strangulation.

Gibby didn't tell him we had other business in the hospital. He just stood pat on his insistence that Bannerman had to be seen by a doctor. We went around the corner and Bannerman, chafing with impatience, came along.

When we hit the receiving room, the doctor in attendance was busy. A cop was in the outer room writing in his notebook. It was no cop either of us knew but he had evidently seen us around. He recognized us and said hello. Gibby asked him if the doc was going to be long.

"Nah," he said. "He's in there with a beat-up drunk I picked up. I found this guy staggering along Madison Avenue and, boy, had he taken a shellacking! Says he got in a fight in a bar somewheres and he don't know what bar or where. Of course, he's lying."

"It does happen in bars once in a while," I said.

The cop laughed. "Not the way I got it figured," he said. "He had this in his hand." He dug in his pocket and brought out a small piece of red lace. "What's that if it ain't a hunk ripped off of some dame's panties? He knows where he was and what he was doing when her husband came home and caught him at it. And you should see the size of him. I'd like to see what that husband looks like."

Gibby took the bit of red stuff out of the cop's hand.

"Watch our boy for a minute, will you?" he said. "He's just been to the morgue on an identification. You know what to do if he faints. We won't be long."

The cop sobered and a look of sympathetic concern came over his ordinarily cheerful face.

"Tough," he murmured. "Relative?"

"Kid sister," Gibby said.

"Gee, tough," said the cop.

We left Bannerman to the officer's tender mercies and went on into the next room. The doctor was in there going like a house afire. He had a man on the table and the man was stripped to the waist. Large areas of him—and this was a man of large areas—were already neatly punctuated with surgical dressings and the doctor was zipping along over this big boy's acreage, cleaning up cuts and abrasions, slapping dressings on them, and making the dressings fast with his neat, white criss-crosses of adhesive tape. The patient lay on the table with his eyes closed. The alcohol on his breath was doing battle with the antiseptic odors of the room and it was almost winning out. Of course, it was the man whose license plate read JERK backwards.

Gibby whispered to the doctor and the doc stepped out of the room with us. We didn't go back to the anteroom where Bannerman was waiting. We went on into another examining room, an empty one.

"Did you say DA's office?" the doc asked.

Gibby gave him the full identification. "How drunk is the big boy?" he asked.

"Not very. He has been drinking. I suppose you could smell it. When they stagger and they smell like that, the police assume it's drunkenness. With him it's more that he's groggy from that pasting he took."

"What are you planning to do with him?"

The doctor shrugged. "When they're like that," he said, "we patch them up and send them home. They always live."

Gibby nodded. "I don't want to put him under arrest

and I haven't time for him right now," he said, "but it would be handy for the DA's office if we could have him on ice for overnight. I'll be ready to take over on him in the morning and he can be turned loose then and no harm done. Could he seem more alcoholic than he is to the extent of a secure night's lodging?"

"We don't have too many beds to spare," the doc said, hesitating.

"I know," Gibby said, "but we don't have too many citizens to spare either. We're working a murder case and we saw him earlier today. He was in better shape then. Turn him loose now and this one just might not live."

"Okay," the doc said. "I'll take him in, but it will be only till morning. By then he's going to look much too sober for us to keep."

"Any time the DA's office can do you a favor," Gibby said.

"No, thanks," the doc answered.

four

The doctor came out to the waiting room with us and gave Bannerman a slug of aromatic spirits of ammonia. Just in the couple of minutes we had left Bannerman alone, a lot of the zip had gone out of him. He had again begun to look as though he could use a pick-me-up. The boy had obviously been thinking and thinking had been doing him no good.

We were in the car and headed uptown before he spoke a word. Then he started asking questions.

"What hotel?" he asked. "I mean where Joanie's staying. I wonder how she found a hotel."

"Moderate priced," Gibby said. "Reasonably decent, very well known. A place called the President Polk."

Bannerman did a double-take on the name. "Did you say President Polk?" he asked.

Gibby nodded. "That where you're staying?" he asked.

It was phrased as a question, but it did sound like one of those questions to which we already knew the answer.

"Yes, but how did you know? I didn't say."

Gibby shrugged. "Miss Loomis from River Forks, Ohio. She doesn't know the town. She wouldn't know the hotels. She has a sudden need of one. I'd expect her to pick the one you were going to be at. She knew you were going in there, didn't she?"

"Yes, of course, she knew."

"No mystery about that then," Gibby said.

Quite suddenly Bannerman looked troubled. "She went there at 9:30 this morning," he said, thinking aloud.

"That was her check-in time," Gibby told him.

"Do they keep a record of those times?" Bannerman asked. His happiness was dimming fast.

"It may not be exact," Gibby said, "but it will be close enough."

"More than six hours after her train from Boston came in. There isn't any place she could have been those six hours. They must be wrong on the time."

"They couldn't be that wrong," Gibby said, speaking as though he were making the point only in the interest of accuracy, as though it weren't of any consequence at all. "Some time shortly after three in the morning would have meant that a night clerk checked her in. The night shift of bellhops would have been on. By 9:30 this morn-ing she would have been received by a completely dif-

94

ferent staff. It's this day staff that has checked out with us on her description."

Bannerman had broken out in a sweat. "Six hours," he muttered. "Six hours when everybody would be alseep, when there would be no place she could possibly have gone."

"She was somewhere," Gibby said.

"But where?" Bannerman wailed.

I took a hand. "Wherever it was," I said, "it's reasonably clear that she came to no harm. She seems to have been in good shape this morning when she did turn up at the hotel. What's to get in a sweat about?"

Bannerman thought awhile. He was in a good deal of a sweat, but he pulled himself together. This, evidently, was going to be a private sweat.

"There will be some perfectly reasonable explanation," he said. "Joanie will be able to explain."

He was trying very hard to sound as though he were believing it, but he didn't seem to be getting very far with convincing even himself.

Gibby spoke to him. His tone was studiedly soothing and reassuring.

"New York," he said, "isn't River Forks. Even after three in the morning you'll find all sorts of people up and around in New York."

Bannerman reacted not at all to the tone. He rose sharply to the words.

"Joanie wouldn't know any of those people," he said firmly. "Joanie doesn't know anybody here except Ellie, and Ellie. . . ."

His voice trailed away from finishing his statement about Ellie.

"She had been here several days before she went up

to Boston," Gibby said. "Your sister had many friends. She had probably gotten to know some of your sister's friends."

Bannerman didn't even want to think about the possibility that his Joanie might have spent those evil hours in this evil city with anyone, however friendly. He came up with a new idea, presenting it hopefully.

"Trains down from Boston?" he asked. "Aren't they ever late?"

"Often," Gibby said and it was that soothing tone again. "Often late. I've known them to be as much as a whole hour late."

If it had been anybody else I might have been wondering whether he knew that he was driving the needle into this worried young man. It was Gibby, however, and since it was Gibby, I couldn't have the first doubt. He not only knew he was giving Bannerman the needle. He knew precisely which nerve he was probing and precisely how far the needle point was going.

We got up to the station and found a place to park and all the time that needle of Gibby's was busy. We didn't go right around to the Incoming Train board to find out on what track they would be bringing in the train from River Forks. We went around to the station master's office instead and checked on the arrival time that morning of the Boston train that had been scheduled for arrival around three o'clock. The information was available and they gave it to us pridefully. That would be the train that had been due in at 2:58. It had been on time.

"Of course," Gibby said, as we were leaving the office, "it does take a bit of time to get off a train and find a cab and all that. It would have been at least 3:15 before she could have been out of the station."

"There will be some perfectly reasonable explanation," Bannerman repeated. This time the statement was made with considerable heat.

"There will have to be," Gibby said.

We were crossing the station to that section at the far end where they post up incoming trains. We had Bannerman walking between us and he wasn't cooling down any. He strode along in a simmering silence.

That bulletin board where they post the trains is at the far end of a large room. As we approached the broad entrance to that room, we saw the man. He was standing in profile to us and both Gibby and I had had a good look at him in profile before he had come out from behind the wheel of his car to talk with us. The recognition hit us both at the same time and automatically we both stopped short. Bannerman, of course, was charging right ahead, but Gibby reached out and pulled him back.

"What's the matter now?" he growled.

"Hold it a sec," Gibby said. "You can see the whole area from here. Is Miss Loomis there?"

Bannerman was straining at the leash but he stood under Gibby's restraining hand and looked carefully over the knot of people collected before the board. There was a shift in the crowd and he jumped forward again.

"There she is," he shouted trying to shake Gibby off. "Right there in front of the board. Let me go."

"In a minute," Gibby said, holding him. "A man right by the entrance. He could be watching her. A man in a brown hat, light brown suit. See him?"

"I don't care about any man," Bannerman growled. I

thought for a minute he was about to swing on Gibby.

"She's there," Gibby snapped. "She's okay. You can see she's okay. You'll get to her soon enough, but first I want you to look at that man. See the one I mean?"

"I see him," Bannerman fumed. "Brown hat, tan suit. What about him?"

"Ever seen him before?"

"How would I have seen him? I don't know a soul in New York."

"You're sure you don't know him?"

"I'm sure. What's all this about?"

"Your sister Ellie. Remember your sister Ellie?"

Bannerman's jaw dropped. "That man?" he gasped.

"Damn it all, Bannerman," Gibby said. "Some man. Look at him. Is he watching the board? Is he looking around as though he were waiting here to meet somebody, or is he just watching Miss Loomis?"

"Who is he?"

Gibby didn't answer the question. "He's our job," Gibby said. "I'm giving you a job, Bannerman, and you're going to have to do this exactly according to instructions. You're going to think I've gone crazy, but take my word for it, I haven't. You're going in there to Miss Loomis. Go in and come up behind her. Don't say a word. Just reach around her from behind and put your hands over her eyes. You know, surprise her."

He did look at Gibby as though he thought Gibby had gone crazy.

"I'll scare her to death," he protested. "Look, she's alone here. She doesn't know anybody. She thinks I won't be here till that train gets in."

"You took that earlier train so you could surprise her," Gibby said, implacably giving Bannerman his orders.

98

"Now you are going to surprise her. You are going to have to follow instructions exactly."

Bannerman moved as though he were trying to break away from Gibby but it was an ineffective try. He seemed to be as curious as he was rebellious.

"I'm not going to do anything of the sort," he said. "I don't have to follow anybody's instructions."

Gibby fixed him with a withering look. "And then when you're up to your ears in trouble," he asked, "where do you plan to turn for help? Your sister's been murdered. You've been half crazy with worry about your girl. Now you see her. She's okay, so you think school's out. Just because nothing's happened to her yet, don't push your luck too far."

Bannerman tried to laugh it off. "I don't know why you're trying to scare me," he said. "I was frightened for Joanie because I thought she had been in the apartment with Ellie and if she had been there, something horrible could have happened to her. It did happen to Ellie, didn't it?"

"Don't bother to remind me," Gibby snapped. "I'm reminding you."

"I haven't forgotten. Luckily Joanie wasn't there, so that's that."

"This man who's watching her doesn't seem to think that's that. We have to know what he's doing here, what he's up to."

"Why don't you ask him? You've asked me plenty of questions. What makes him immune?"

"We'll take care of him, but you're going to set it up for us. We've got the job of catching up with your sister's killer. I can see that you don't care a damn about that."

"That's a lie."

"You can convince me by co-operating and you had better also remember that it's our job to prevent any further killings if we can. Protecting Miss Loomis is at least as important as any other part of this thing."

"Joanie will be all right now. I'll take care of protecting her."

Gibby shook his head sadly. "And then we'll end up protecting you, too," he said. "Can't you just assume that we know what we're doing and play along?"

"When you ask me to play a silly practical joke . . ."

"Stop thinking," Gibby snapped, "and do as you're told. You go up quietly behind her and put your hands over her eyes. That's all you have to do. After that just take her over there where it says Waiting Room. Go in there with her and wait till we come and get you. While you're waiting, you tell her nothing. Your story is that you came in early to surprise the girls. You went around to your sister's and there was no answer to the bell. You've been trying over there ever since and no answer, so, as train time approached, you came over here just on the chance that she would be here. If she wasn't you were going back to your sister's and try again, figuring that they would certainly be home by then since it was the time they would have been expecting you. Now that isn't difficult. You can do that, can't you?"

Scowling, Bannerman shook his head in emphatic refusal. "I do not tell lies," he said and he couldn't have summoned up more indignation if Gibby had tried to suborn him to perjury. "I don't know what you're after or how important it may be to you, but this is important to me. Joanie and I have a lifetime ahead of us. I don't blemish it now by lying to her."

"Okay," Gibby growled. "Have it your own way. I was going to give you a break, let you have a couple of moments alone with your girl. You don't want it that way, so you can have your couple of moments alone with her and a police officer."

"You can't do that," Bannerman protested.

"Unless I have your oath that you will follow my instructions," Gibby said coldly, "I'll do exactly that."

Bannerman hesitated. He studied Gibby's face for a moment. It was absolutely stony. He turned to me. I put everything I had into making mine as granitic as Gibby's. I must have succeeded. Bannerman caved in. He did bargain a bit, but we had him.

"I make one condition," he said. "If I am to lie to Joanie, I'll be doing it under duress. You will tell her that. You forced me to lie to her."

"We'll tell her," Gibby promised. "We forced you to lie to her. We know more about how to handle these things than you can know or she can know, but even in the face of that you didn't want to lie to her. You did it for the only reason that could ever have moved you, the fact that her safety and maybe her life are at stake."

Bannerman sighed. "I don't know why I believe you," he said, "but I do. I'll follow your instructions."

Gibby let go his arm and slapped him on the shoulder. "Good boy," he said. "Go to her now."

Bannerman took off. When he had first seen her, he had been ready to take off on the run. Now he went with dragging feet. The task Gibby had set him was evidently so distasteful that it was quite outweighing his eagerness.

"Do you think he's going to do as you told him?" 1 asked.

"That," Gibby said, "depends on whether he's scared enough to go against his principles. We have to risk it."

As he spoke he was moving slowly off to the left. I moved with him. I could see what he was doing. He was keeping in position so that he had the man in the tan suit and brown hat, Bannerman, and the girl all lined up in front of him. He was watching all of them at once. The man didn't move around much, only as much as was necessary so that he could keep his eye always on Joan Loomis. I didn't even for a moment have the thought that we might be mistaken. There was no question about it. This was the man who had driven Kirk Reginald Emmenthal Jellicoe away from our encounter in front of that secondhand-clothing store.

"You know," I murmured, "we're going out on so many limbs today that I'm losing count. We've tangled with this baby once before and got out of it luckily. We're holding Jellicoe down at Bellevue on the phoniest of phonies and now I don't even want to think about when the time will come around and you'll have to explain all this to Bannerman. He's the righteous type. If he catches you cutting corners, he'll take it to the Old Man. That's not a boy who believes in forgiveness for sin."

"I'm betting he'll have to do his explaining first," Gibby said. "Anyhow we can worry later. Watch this now."

We watched. Bannerman came quietly up behind the girl. He put his hands over her eyes. Her reaction time was the quickest I've ever seen. It was as though he had pulled a trigger. She whirled around and with a full swing of arm and body she slapped him. That was a

102

slap. The crack of it echoed and re-echoed in that vast marble enclosure. Bannerman rocked on his heels and touched his hand to his reddened cheek. Then and only then, the girl screamed.

"Milty. No, Milty, you're not here. Your train isn't in yet."

We were in luck. We could see his face full on. Since he didn't scream back at her we couldn't hear but we could watch his lips and read them. Lip reading ordinarily isn't one of Gibby's talents nor is it one of mine but when you have a pretty good idea of what a man might say, you can make a good stab at telling whether the lip movements fit with what you think he's saying.

"I got away earlier than I thought I could."

If those weren't the exact words, they came very close.

Since all he said was that or something very like it, I was completely unprepared for her next move. After the violence of her immediate reaction to the shock he had given her, I was all the more unprepared for it. She swayed dizzily and reached a hand out toward him. Before she touched him, however, the hand wavered and she dropped at his feet and lay there. Joan Loomis had fainted.

Gibby laughed. "That's all I wanted to know."

Practically everybody within fifty feet was now converging on Bannerman and the girl. You know how people are. Anything like that happens and in no time you have a crowd gathered around it. Our friend in the brown hat didn't move. He did keep a sharp eye on the gathering crowd but he showed no inclination toward joining it.

"I'm stupid," I said. "Fill me in. What did that get us?"

"It got us the information that Miss Loomis' nerves are in a state where they go off like firecrackers. Her reaction to hands coming around her unexpectedly is quick and violent, but her reaction to any deviation from timetable is worse than that—catastrophic at least."

It was an answer of sorts. I tabled it for later consideration and tried another question.

"Our friend in the brown hat," I said, "is interested but it's a most aloof interest. Do you like that, too?"

"It has me enthralled," Gibby said. "Let's go."

I didn't quite know where we were going but Gibby moved and I moved with him. We moved in on brown hat. Coming up alongside him, Gibby gave it the jolly good-fellowship touch.

"What made Mae's party go sour?" he asked.

If Joan Loomis had demonstrated the jumpiness of her nerves, the man in the brown hat wasn't far behind. He jumped a country mile. I think his first impulse was to cut and run but he stood fast and let us watch him take a grip on himself.

"Oh," he said, half strangling on the words. "It's you again."

"Some days it's like that," Gibby said. "Even in a town as big as this, you keep bumping into the same people wherever you go."

"Yeah," the man muttered. " 'Specially in Grand Central Station. Great spot for meeting people, Grand Central Station."

"You're meeting someone?" Gibby asked.

"The big boy. I've been worrying about him."

"You mean Jellicoe?"

The man laughed. "You did think I was kidnaping him," he said. "I can see you've been checking up. There's one comfort anyhow. Whatever he's doing, the drunken bastard isn't driving. We've got his car."

"Last we saw, you had him. How'd he get away from you?"

The man shrugged. "I still got a lot to learn," he said. "He tells me he's got to go to the john. If I was smart I would have gone in with him but do you figure a drunk, he's going to be so tricky, he'll find a john it's got two entrances? I wait where he went in but that ain't where he comes out, the tricky son-of-a-bitch."

"And after he went to all that trouble to shake you, you're expecting him to keep a date here?"

"He don't know we got a date," the man said. "I'm probably wasting my time. Maybe he won't go home to Connecticut at all. Maybe he'll get in a taxi and ride that way all the way to the country. If it's like that, there's nothing I can do about it; but there's just the chance. Not having his car, he might take the train. He comes here to take the train, I pick him up."

Gibby grinned. "How do you know he's that drunk?" he asked. "What makes you think he's drunk enough to go out on an incoming train?"

I expected he would have to spell that out before he could have any answer to it, but I was wrong. The man caught it on the first bounce.

"I check every train that goes out to his neck of the woods," the man explained. "Between trains this is as good a place to wait as any. I can't watch all the entrances to the lower level where them commuters' trains go out, but that over there is one way in."

"That over there" was an entrance to the station's lower level, but it was a direction to which the man had kept his back steadily turned up to the time when Gibby had accosted him. So far as I could determine, he was facing that way now only because he'd had to turn to talk to us.

"What do you want with Jellicoe?" Gibby asked.

"I want to take him home if I can. Even Jellicoe sobers up for a while in the morning. He sobers up and you've been taking care of him, he's grateful. That's always a nice piece of change, Jellicoe's gratitude."

"Better than rolling him when he's drunk?" Gibby asked.

The man started to take offense at that question. I was ready to predict every word he would say, all the protestations that he was being misjudged. I have a hunch that he read it in our faces that we were way ahead of him. He switched away from any pretensions to innocence.

"A lot better," he said. "You can roll a drunk, sure, and what have you got? A one-time shot. Gratitude can happen all the time, again and again and again. It can be as good as a meal ticket."

Gibby nodded. "Worth the effort," he said. "But you have to work at it. Jellicoe could have gone by you a dozen times while you were busy giving the dame the eye."

"I suppose. I was trying to make up my mind. That's a real nice-looking little tomato. I'm thinking maybe I'll say to hell with Jellicoe and have a try at making that. If you seen me giving her the eye, you also seen what happened to the guy who did try to make her. I saw that, it put my mind back on Jellicoe, but who can blame me for thinking about it? Like they say, all work and no play makes Jack a dull boy."

Gibby laughed. "Okay, Jack," he said. "We'll be seeing you."

Joan Loomis had been revived. She was on her feet and Bannerman was helping her toward the waiting room. Her walking was a bit rubber-kneed but she was managing all right. She had a station policeman supporting her on the other side.

We strolled off after them. A handful of the crowd she had gathered was also strolling that way. The rest of the people were reluctantly taking off to meet those trains they had come to meet.

"How did we do with brown hat?" I asked.

"You can't win all the time," Gibby said.

"We lost on that one?"

"Gave as much as we got."

Going through the big main rotunda of the station we made a small detour before going into the waiting room to join Bannerman and his girl. Gibby stopped at the information desk to pick up the New Haven timetable, the big one that lists all the line's trains in and out of New York. Dropping it into his pocket, he made for the waiting room.

The minute we came up to the bench where Bannerman and the cop had settled the white-faced Miss Loomis, Bannerman rounded on us angrily. It seemed to me that we had done just about as well in this quarter as we had with Jellicoe's self-appointed bodyguard. Here too, I thought, we had given as much as we got. Gibby could be as pleased as he liked with the bits of information he had drawn out of that little drama he had staged, but for those bits it looked as though we were going to have to pay the price of Bannerman's hostility. Any further co-operation we might need from that lad I was ready to write off as a dead loss. He had done all the co-operating we could expect of him. He said as much.

"That was a dandy idea of yours," he snarled. "It was one jim-dandy."

Of course, the original expectation had been that if he did follow instructions he would end up resentful of us because of the burden that would have been laid on his conscience by Gibby's requirement that he lie to his Joanie. Now, of course, that part of it was quite all right. He had had no time to tell her anything, whether true or false. Her faint had taken care of that part of it. That faint, however, I hadn't foreseen any more than I had foreseen the slap in the jaw, and now it was for those we were being blamed. Actually it was because of the girl's fainting that Bannerman was angry with us even though moment by moment she was making a better recovery from that than he was making from the slap. Even as he harangued us, the color was coming back into her face. The mark of her hand on his face wasn't fading that fast. She had really let him have it.

Gibby let Bannerman blow off his steam. He said nothing until Bannerman had paused for breath and even then Gibby made no direct answer. Bypassing Bannerman, Gibby spoke to the girl. He introduced himself and he introduced me. He explained that we were from the DA's office.

"Did you know that you were being followed?" he asked.

"Followed? What do you mean followed?"

"A man was following you."

She shuddered. "Oh, that," she said. "Everywhere I go in this horrible town it happens. Men follow me or they look at me as though they were trying to hypnotize me or something or they come right up to me and ask me where I'm going and can't they help me find it. Don't New York men have anything else to do? Do they have their whole day free for bothering women?"

"Some make a career of it," Gibby said. "Then you knew that a man followed you into the station, that you were being watched all the time?"

"If it wasn't one man it was another. I didn't notice that there was a man just then but they've got me so jumpy, all of them, that when Milton came up behind me and put his hands over my eyes, it never occurred to me that it could be anything but another one. That's why I slapped him. I didn't care who it was. I wanted to tear his eyes out."

"Yes," Gibby said. "We saw you. I must apologize. It was my idea. I wanted to make that fellow who had been following you commit himself. I am sorry, particularly since it didn't work. He didn't commit himself at all."

"Commit himself how?"

"Any way at all. I'm afraid you have been in danger, Miss Loomis, and I can't be certain that you are not still in danger. The more we know about the nature of this danger, the better we can head it off."

She reached out her hand to Bannerman. He took it and held it.

"I've been in danger," she said, "and I can tell you exactly what the danger is. I'm with Milton now. I'll be all right."

"We have to be certain of that," Gibby insisted. "We

can't take any chances with your safety. What was the danger, Miss Loomis?"

"N-e-w Y-o-r-k," she said, spelling it out for him letter by letter. "New York. This is a terrible place. Maybe if a girl knows it, she can learn how to cope with it—all those awful men—but I don't think I could ever learn to cope and I can tell you I'm mighty glad I don't have to try. Milton's with me now and we're going home to River Forks just as fast as ever we can. If I never see this place again, it will be too soon."

Gibby turned to Bannerman. "Fainting the way she did," he said, "she's probably hungry. Do you know? Has she had any dinner?"

Bannerman turned to the girl.

"Of course, I had dinner," she said. "I found a place. It isn't far from here, as a matter of fact, and it's clean and quite expensive enough. It was almost two o'clock before I found that because I didn't know where to go. The places Ellie goes, Milt, they're simply awful. When I tried to find something for myself, all the places I looked at were bad enough till I found this one."

There was a small misunderstanding there but it wasn't of any consequence. River Forks, of course, dined at midday, but Gibby passed that by. He was more interested in these places Ellie went, the awful ones. He asked about them.

"They all had bars in them," Miss Loomis explained. "Drinking places. Of course, we didn't drink, but still. No matter when you went in, there would be people drinking, women and men, women just by themselves even, drinking. But it's the prices. The prices are simply scandalous. There's a thing they call chef's salad Ellie's always eating and it's nothing but a lot of lettuce and stuff like that and it has a little bit of cut-up chicken in it. They cut it up fine and spread it around to make it look as though there were really a decent lot of chicken, but if they have twenty-five cents' worth of chicken in the whole thing, that's a lot, and do you know what they charge for it? Just guess."

We let Bannerman guess. He guessed a dollar.

Miss Loomis laughed bitterly. "Two dollars and fifty cents," she said. "And that isn't all. They charge separately for bread and butter and Ellie never eats any. She doesn't touch it but she pays for it all the same, bread and butter she doesn't even eat. It's really too awful."

"It sure is," Gibby said, "but people do have to eat. I know what's wrong with you, young woman. Even though you did find this place at two o'clock, you didn't eat nearly enough and now it's long past your supper time. You're starved. That's your trouble."

I'm not going to go into all the to-do we had about getting them out of the station and over to a restaurant where we could both eat and talk. This place she had found that didn't shock her too much was the Automat, and even the medium-priced place Gibby selected scandalized both her and Milton. They didn't like being in a place with a bar and the prices were against their principles even though we were paying.

We finally got them to order something and Gibby was able to settle in to asking questions. He started out by telling the girl that we had been very much worried about her.

"We didn't know where you had gotten off to," he said. "Milton, here, called your cousin in Boston and she said you left there last night and should have arrived here about three this morning. That scared us all the more."

The girl sighed. "Poor Milt," she said. "I can just imagine. It was terribly silly of me insisting on taking that late train last night. I know that now, but I couldn't even dream that I'd get to Ellie's and she wouldn't be there. I can't think where she's gone and I do think it isn't very nice of her either, Milt."

Bannerman started to explain but Gibby cut him off.

"You went around to her apartment when the train came in?" Gibby asked quickly.

"Of course. Where else would I go? I was staying there with her, and it wasn't as though she didn't know I was coming back from Boston. She knew I was coming and she told me it didn't matter what train I came down on. She was going to be at the apartment and any time at all she'd be there to let me in and then she wasn't and it was after three in the morning."

"Hadn't she given you a key?" Gibby asked.

"No, she hadn't and even if she was called away overnight, she did know that Milt was coming in this evening and it had been planned that he would go directly to her place. I should think that she would have managed to get back there by this afternoon, at least. I can't understand her being so inconsiderate."

Gibby was right in there with his next question but Bannerman was in there, too. There hadn't been any hope of keeping him shut up indefinitely.

"Ellie's dead, Joanie," he said.

The girl clutched at him. "Dead," she moaned. "Oh, no, Milty, she can't be. It's only a couple of days since I left her to go to Boston and she was perfectly well. What happened to her?"

"She died suddenly," Gibby said, while Bannerman was casting around for words.

"Accident? This awful traffic, the taxis and the buses and the trucks and the cars. It frightens me half to death."

Bannerman found his words. There wasn't anything we could do about it.

"She was killed," he said. "A burglar came in while she was asleep and strangled her."

The girl rallied. Abruptly she wasn't thinking of herself at all. She was all concern for Bannerman. "Darling," she murmured, stroking his hand. "Poor, poor darling. How awful for you. How incredibly awful for you."

Gibby stepped into it and tried to put the thing back under control.

"Now you can understand why we were so worried about you," he said. "As I understand it, you went to her place straight from your train last night and you rang her bell."

"Yes," she said and turned back to Bannerman. "I know that sounds a very strange thing to do. You know, I'd never do anything like that back home, but you can't imagine how different things are here in New York. Ellie often sleeps right through to noon or even into the afternoon. That's the way it is here. Night's like day and day's like night. Why, her friends think nothing of telephoning her at the craziest hours. Three in the morning. Four in the morning. And it's not only her friends. It's her job, too. One night while I was with her, the phone rang way after two. Ellie just sat up in bed and answered it. If the phone rings in the night that way back home people get frightened half to death. They can't think anything but that there's been an accident or something like that, but Ellie never seemed to mind in the least. Sometimes she'd talk awhile and then go back to sleep. This one time though and it was almost three, she made an appointment and she got up and dressed and went out. She told me to go back to sleep and not worry about her. She had to go to work. At that time of night, imagine. It was something about sunrise pictures. They were photographing her hands against the sunrise. I think it was for a perfume, something that used some slogan about lovely as a morning sunrise. It seemed crazy to me but there's so much that happens here that is just beyond understanding."

Bannerman was shaking his head. It was evidently as much beyond his understanding as it was beyond hers. Gibby played along, pretending that it was somewhat beyond his understanding as well.

"Particularly," he said dryly, "since they could have gotten the same effect at sunset if they did it standing on their heads."

"Of course," Miss Loomis continued, "they were paying her fantastic amounts for posing for these pictures but after I'd been here a couple of days, I began to think she earned it, getting up out of a deep sleep to have her hands photographed against the sunrise. It's really too silly."

"You said she made an appointment," Gibby asked. "Could you by any chance remember anything of the conversation, where she was going for these pictures, who called her, anything like that?"

The girl shook her head. "No," she said. "She never spoke much on the telephone. Mostly she listened and said yes or no or later or tomorrow."

114

Gibby nodded. "Yes," he said. "It figures. So you went around to her place from the train and rang her bell. What happened then?"

She began talking and, warming to her story, she was off in full spate. We just sat back and listened. She had rung the bell and when there was no answer she had rung again. She had kept ringing for a long time and then she had realized that it couldn't be that Ellie Bannerman was upstairs in bed and so tight asleep that she wasn't hearing the bell. She always heard the telephone bell and the doorbell was just as loud. She assumed that it had been another call for sunrise photos and Ellie had been forced to leave in a hurry.

"I couldn't imagine that she wouldn't have left me a note in the letter box or something," she said. "But I thought she must have been too much in a hurry and had taken the chance that I wouldn't be in till morning and that she would be home by then."

As she went on with her story I could sense the disbelief that was growing and blossoming inside Gibby. It wasn't merely that my own credulity was straining at the seams with the tax this little miss was putting on it. I know Gibby well enough so that I can always tell when that extra edge of alertness begins to manifest itself. He wasn't showing it to the girl or to Bannerman, but it was there. I've known it to come at times when I can't even guess what might be bringing it on but this time I didn't have to guess. The story of that young woman's movements after she had rung Ellie Bannerman's bell in the wee hours of the morning defied belief. The fact that to all seeming it sounded completely reasonable to Milton Bannerman wasn't making it ring any truer for me.

She couldn't hang around in that vestibule until morning. She had to go somewhere and she didn't know any place in New York that she could go that time of night. Then she remembered a place—back to the railway station. She carried her bags out to the street and hailed a late cruising cab. Back in Grand Central Station, she settled herself in the waiting room and stayed there till morning. At about half-hour intervals she telephoned the apartment, but there was never an answer.

By nine, she lost patience. Even if it had been a hands-against-the-sunrise job, Ellie should have been home from it long since. The sunrise was then hours gone. Joan Loomis gave up on trying to reach Sister Ellie. She had gone around to the hotel and taken a room.

"Wouldn't it have been more sensible to go directly to a hotel and get some sleep instead of sitting up the rest of the night in the station?" Gibby asked.

"If I had known I was going to have to have a room anyhow," the girl answered. "But I didn't know and I wasn't going to spend that kind of money for nothing."

Bannerman nodded approvingly. This was a matter of thrift and it was obvious that thrift came in that same package with not smoking and not drinking. It was a part of decency. Gibby was not so easily satisfied. He had a dozen questions and before he was through, he had explored the young woman's thinking exhaustively.

She had expected that Milton's sister would certainly be returning home before nightfall, but she could explain quite to her own and Milton's satisfaction why she had refrained from paying for a hotel room for the night when she had needed one, only to take one the next day when she had no expectation of needing it. It hadn't been a matter of expectation. It had been a matter of immediate necessity. She had been all night in her clothes. She had to have a bath and a change. She had to have a place where later in the day she could freshen up to meet Milty. She was ashamed to admit it, now that she knew how unjust she had been to Ellie, but she had even been a little angry with her future sister-in-law, angry enough to feel that there would have to be a very good explanation indeed before she would ever want to go back to the apartment again.

"So angry," Gibby said, "that you even stopped phoning her. You decided you'd meet Milt's train and let her worry awhile."

"Oh, no," Joanie said quickly. "I kept right on calling. I've been calling all day. It wasn't more than ten minutes before you found me over there in the station that I called the last time. Just about every half hour all day I tried her phone and never an answer."

That one gave even Bannerman pause. Gibby didn't have to ask the question. Bannerman was in there asking it for him.

"But what number were you calling, Joanie?" he asked. "We were in the apartment for a long time this afternoon and the police had been there before I arrived."

Joanie gave him the great big baby stare. "You were there?" she exclaimed. "And you let the telephone ring and ring? Didn't it even occur to you that it would be me calling?"

"But it didn't ring at all. What number were you calling?"

"Ellie's number," she said.

She reeled it off and Bannerman relaxed.

"You had it wrong all the time," he said. "It isn't 0913. It's 0912."

The baby stare held, but now her mouth opened to match the round astonishment of her eyes. She repeated the two numbers after him.

"You're sure it's 0912?" she asked.

Bannerman brought out a little address book and showed her the number.

"That's what comes of missing a whole night's sleep," he said.

"Oh, dear," she sighed. "All night and all day I've been calling the wrong number."

Gibby excused himself and left the table. He crossed the restaurant to a telephone booth. He wasn't gone long. All the time he was gone Joan Loomis went on and on about how stupid she had been, making all those calls and all to the wrong number. They could have been together so much sooner if she just hadn't been such an idiot.

Bannerman took out his handkerchief and mopped his face. "You'll never make a better mistake, darling," he said. "This afternoon would have been all right. You would have gotten the police or me, but before that—I don't even want to think who might have answered before that."

She shuddered and he took her hand in his and stroked it gently.

Gibby came back to the table and sat down.

"On all these calls you made," he said, "you never got an answer? Not a wrong number answering or anything like that? Just no answer at all?"

"No answer ever."

118

"Funny," Gibby said. "I just called 0913. I got a Mrs. Hastings who stood on a chair last week to reach something down from a high shelf. She fell and broke her leg. She's been home all week with her leg in a cast and she always answers her telephone because she's so lonely and bored that even a wrong number is a diversion. She said her phone rang only twice in the last twenty-four hours. Once it was her brother calling and the other time her best friend."

Joan Loomis giggled nervously. "Oh dear, oh dear," she said. "I wasn't even dialing the wrong number right. I suppose I've been more nervous and confused than I realized. How very silly."

five

It was silly and it got sillier. We could have been working two completely different murders. We had formed our picture of the dead girl, a picture compounded from what we'd had from Nora McGuire and what the cleaning woman had given us. I can't say that there weren't the odd bits which would not fit in with that picture. There was the prayer book. There were the religious tracts. There was the relatively austere red flannel nightgown and there were the relatively sexless underthings. Odd as they had been, however, that had not been too disquieting. There were conceivable patterns into which they could have been fitted and we could hope that the very process of finding the proper fit for them could easily lead to breaking the case.

Milton Bannerman's picture of the dead girl, however, had at every point been at odds with our original idea of her. His description of his sister fitted with nothing but what had previously been our odd bits—the prayer book, the tracts, the red flannel nightgown, those under-clothes which the cleaning woman's daughter wouldn't touch with a ten-foot pole. That discrepancy, however, had not been too difficult to explain. Milton Bannerman had never been in New York before. The Ellie he had known had been a River Forks girl, and the River Forks' Ellie Bannerman had been quite unlike New York's Sydney Bell. Ellie had changed but she had never wanted her brother to know anything of the change. Each time she had gone back to River Forks to visit him she had for the occasion resumed her River Forks ways and her River Forks personality. How could he have known what Sydney Bell was really like? So far as he had been allowed to know, that had been the whole ex-tent of the change. His sister had assumed a profes-sional name for her modeling. Otherwise she had con-tinued to be the little Ellie he had always known.

Joan Loomis, on the other hand, was very much something else again. She had come to New York. She had stayed with Milt's sister, had shared the one-room apartment, shared the double bed. In the face of all that, nevertheless, she seemed to be quite as deluded about Sydney Bell as was brother Milton. She knew the red flannel nightdress well. She thought it was sweet. It was the one Ellie had been using when Joan had been with her.

Gibby hauled out of his pocket the torn hunk of lace he had taken over from the policeman at Bellevue. He laid it on the table in front of the girl. She looked at it, studying it as though she had never seen lace before.

"Isn't that pretty?" she said politely.

"Too bad it's torn," Gibby murmured.

She nodded and turned to Bannerman. "You find lace all over things in the stores here," she said, "and it's shocking the prices they charge for it, especially since it's so impractical."

Bannerman gave her an approving smile. Beyond that, however, he behaved as though he couldn't have cared less.

"Was that hers?" Gibby asked.

"Whose?" Joanie said.

"Sydney Bell's, Ellie Bannerman's, your future sister-in-law's."

"I don't know. She may have had a dress or a blouse with lace on it. You know, a lace collar or something like that. But it wouldn't be like this. She wouldn't have red lace."

"This probably came off underwear," Gibby said. "Pants or a nightgown, one of those things. You'll know better about them than we can."

The girl blushed a pretty pink. "Oh, no," she said. "I do know about those things. I've seen them in the stores, but Ellie never wore anything like that. Ellie has very nice things."

With Gibby in there pushing, she gave us a description of Ellie's "nice things." Believe it or not, I actually recognized some of the stuff from her descriptions, suits and a coat that had been hanging in the closet back at the apartment, nothing like the garments the cleaning woman had shown us, nothing like the pretties that had caught Nora McGuire's eye.

"Did you ever see her pink satin evening coat?" Gibby asked.

"Pink satin?" She gave it careful thought. "I know I never saw anything like that," she said. "I don't know that I've seen all her things but I doubt very much that she would have owned a pink satin coat. It wouldn't have been at all like Ellie." She turned to Bannerman for corroboration. "You know how she dressed, Milt," she said. "She did have nice things but nothing showy or vulgar. Pink satin, why, that sounds—it sounds . . ." She paused, fumbling for the word.

Bannerman came up with it for her. "It sounds chorus-girly," he said. "I've been telling you Ellie wasn't anything like that."

Gibby scooped the red lace up off the table and stowed it away. He seemed to be changing the subject. Knowing the score as well as I did, I realized that he wasn't. He asked the Loomis girl when she had first arrived in town, how long she had been with Ellie before she left for Boston, whether she had ever seen Ellie's cleaning woman or the girl who lived in 5E.

She hadn't seen the cleaning woman but she had heard about her. She knew that Ellie had been having her twice a week and what her days were. The woman had been in the day before Joanie arrived and had been due again the day Joanie had left for Boston, but Joanie had been out to catch her morning train before the woman had turned up. Joanie had never run into the girl in 5E.

I could see what Gibby was after. He was trying to close the loopholes, to make quite certain that we were indeed faced with a contradiction. We couldn't ignore the possibility that Sydney Bell had been every bit the party girl her neighbor and her cleaning woman thought her to be and that, being what she was, she had nevertheless done the complete job of keeping any knowledge of it from her brother, even to getting out of sight before Joanie arrived any of the things that might have given the people from River Forks a clue—all her clothing except for the few suitably austere items, her liquor, her cigarettes, her ash trays, her New York friends and acquaintances.

It did seem as though she had done exactly that. There was only one small detail which loomed as an obstacle to believing it. Joan Loomis had been three days with Ellie in New York and then three days in Boston. On the very day when she had taken off for Boston the cleaning woman had later been in the apartment and had on that day seen all the fripperies which one day would have been Gloria's. In other words we either had to make a choice between believing such evidence as we had from our New York witnesses and the testimony of our River Forks witnesses, or else we had to believe that Sydney Bell had removed all evidence of the gay life before Joan Loomis arrived on her visit, had brought it all back the first moment Joan was out of the apartment and had then whisked it away again in preparation for Joan's return and Milton Bannerman's arrival.

Since the Bell girl had been dead more than twenty-four hours before her body had been discovered and since she had been found dressed in that red flannel deal and with her place stripped of all the fripperies, there arose an important question. Why would she bring back all that stuff for such a very brief time? She would have had to be extraordinarily quick in bringing it back before her cleaning woman came that day the Loomis girl had taken off for Boston, but then it did look as though she might have been extraordinarily previous in getting it out of the apartment again.

I had known all along that Gibby was working along those lines and his next question did demonstrate that for this particular stretch of the course we had been thinking with one mind. He asked little Loomis whether she had told Ellie exactly when to expect her back from Boston.

"Not exactly," Joan answered. "We knew Milt would be in tonight and I said I would come back the day before because I wanted another day for shopping here. I said I would take an afternoon train and she said I could come in any time. She would be home. She said it would be all right if I wanted to stay in Boston a little longer. I could come in any time, no matter how late. That's what encouraged me to take that late train."

Part of it was answering Gibby and part of it was addressed more to Bannerman. Ellie had urged her not to hurry her Boston visit, had told her that she could come down from Boston even on the day when Milton was expected since he wasn't to be in before evening. Joan explained that she would have planned it that way in the first place except that she had wanted that day for shopping, but then in Boston she had found this store where the basement shop had all the things she wanted and such very good values that she had actually done all her shopping in Boston and could easily have stayed over the extra night, coming down on a daytime train, except that she had been so emphatic with Ellie in telling her that she was coming back to shop that she had thought Ellie might worry about her if she did spend the extra night.

"That was part of the reason I was angry with poor Ellie when she didn't answer the bell," she said. "I had worn myself out on that horrid night train only because I hadn't wanted her to worry about me and then it did seem to me as though she had been so little concerned that she had gone out without even giving a thought to where I would sleep the night."

Gibby waited patiently till she had quite finished. She had subsided into silence and she was just sitting there wearing a faintly rueful look. It was the look of a girl who was blaming herself for having entertained harsh thoughts unjustly. Bannerman recognized the look for that. He patted her hand and murmured at her comfortingly.

When Gibby spoke, he was also murmuring. "You had finished your shopping in that Boston bargain basement," he said. "What were you buying all day today?"

The girl flushed and dropped her eyes. She stole a sidelong glance at Bannerman and was fetched up short by the look of puzzled distress Gibby's words had brought into his face. She dropped her eyes again. Gibby didn't have to prod her. Bannerman did it for him.

"That's right, Joanie," he said, speaking with the gentle severity of a father who is bent on leading an erring child back to the path of righteousness. "You were shopping today. They said at the hotel that you were out all day and came back with your arms full of parcels."

The girl rallied. She turned on him a really enchanting look of mingled guilt and mischief.

"I do try so hard to be sensible," she said. "And

most of the time I am, but I am a girl and we are about to be married and I don't know if I'll ever be any place again where there are so many stores and so many things to buy. I did lose my head a little, having the whole day and Ellie not home and nothing to do until you came. I went out just to look. Ellie used to call it window-shopping, but then I just couldn't resist things and I did buy some things I had never planned to buy and I really don't need. It's awful, I know, but it is such fun just once being foolish about money."

The severity faded out of Bannerman's expression, and he was left with a look that had in it nothing but gentle indulgence. There was, after all, no other way he could look. The girl was being as cute as a button. I shot a glance at Gibby. He's no less prey than the rest of us to most of the charming feminine attributes, but he has never gone for cuteness. A very little cuteness lasts Gibby a long time. He was looking sour. Quickly he changed over to looking dead-pan.

Shifting his line of questioning, he worked over the area of Sydney Bell's friends, her acquaintances, her business associations. He had come on completely arid ground. There was that faintly rueful embarrassment again. Joan Loomis had been thinking ill of the dead and it was not at all nice to think ill of the dead even if there had been no way of knowing that death was on the way.

Ellie, she said, did have friends. She felt quite certain that Ellie lived a very busy social life when she was alone in New York. It wasn't only that she had always assured them that she wasn't lonely in the big city, that she never wanted for friends. It was more than that.

Her telephone rang frequently and she had been on intimate terms with all her callers.

"Everybody that called," Joan said, "she was always calling them darling."

"Men or women?" Gibby asked.

The question took the girl aback. "Women, of course," she said. "I told you she called them darling and she wouldn't be saying that to a man unless she was engaged to him and we would have known if she had been engaged." She turned to Bannerman. "She would have told you," she asked, "wouldn't she?"

"She would have told me," Bannerman said. "It was a burglar who found her there asleep."

Gibby ignored him. He kept after the girl. He asked if she had ever had occasion to answer the telephone. She had not.

"I had the feeling all along that she was ashamed of me," she said, speaking directly at Bannerman, explaining her feelings to him. "She didn't want her New York friends to know anything about the simple country girl her brother was marrying."

"You know Ellie wasn't like that," Bannerman protested.

"I kept telling myself she wasn't, but I couldn't help that feeling. She had all these friends but she never asked anyone in to meet me. She never took me anyplace where we met anyone she knew. Why, up in Boston, they had practically the whole city in when I was with them. That's why I stayed over till that late train. They were heartbroken at the thought of my going off and not meeting these friends they had over last night. I couldn't help feeling that the way they did in Boston was the more natural way. It was just what we would do at home. This down here was so strange, so different. She didn't even want me so much as picking up the phone for her. Even if she was in her shower, she would come out the minute it rang and it wasn't as though she didn't want me bothered. She would definitely tell me not to pick it up. She would be out to answer it. And you know it isn't as though she had to live here or had to associate with the people she knows here. She could always come home to River Forks. You know that. So she must like the people and she couldn't possibly be ashamed of them. I just couldn't understand it any other way, Milt. She was ashamed of me."

"No, that's nonsense," Bannerman insisted. "Ellie adored you."

"Oh, she couldn't have been sweeter," Joan said quickly. "She couldn't do too much for me. When I'd price things in the stores and they were so dreadfully high and I wanted to look around some more because there would have to be some place where you could get good values, why, I almost had to fight with her because she was always arguing that I should buy myself these fantastically expensive things and let her pay for them. If I had let her do it, she would have bought out whole stores and heaped the things on me. It was just that she kept me hidden away from everybody."

"Since everybody included a strangler," Gibby said, "maybe she knew what she was doing."

Joan sighed. "It's all so bewildering," she said. "It's horrible but it's bewildering, too."

"Fingernails," Gibby said.

Both Bannerman and the girl looked at him. It was

evident that they wanted to suggest that a comment of that sort made a confusing affair no less confused.

"What about fingernails?" Bannerman asked.

"How did she wear hers?"

"How would she wear them?" Bannerman asked witheringly. "Clean, of course."

"Was she in the habit of biting them?"

Joan Loomis answered that one. "Oh, no," she said. "That was her job, having people take pictures of her hands. She took the most extraordinary care of her hands. She had to."

"Let's see yours," Gibby said.

Joan put her hands out. She looked like a child who had come to table and been asked if she had remembered to wash her hands. She had remembered. They were like the rest of her, a very nice pair of hands. The nails were short and neatly rounded and they were the color and texture that nature made them. There was no lacquer or polish on them.

"Mine aren't anything," she said. "Ellie's were beautiful."

"All polished and colored?" Gibby asked.

Bannerman shook his head. He didn't like the idea at all and he wanted it quickly put out of the way.

Joan spoke. "Only when she had to," she said. "Sometimes she did have to have them all fancied up. If it was to be an advertisement for manicure stuff, she would have to have all that gop on them, but the rest of the time she had them done like mine."

"As long as yours are?" Gibby asked.

"Mine aren't long," the girl said with noticeable indignation.

"Hers were longer?"

"No. They were like mine."

"Shorter?"

"Only if she had just done them and then they might be a little shorter."

"Never painfully short?"

"Of course not. That would be ugly and the people who took pictures of her hands wouldn't want them."

Assuming that Gibby would be through with his examination of her hands, Joan started to put them back in her lap. Gibby reached across the table and took hold of them.

"We'll be needing your fingerprints," he said. "Have you ever had your prints taken?"

Bannerman came in angrily. "She hasn't," he said. "And she's not going to have it done now. We've had more than enough of this. I can't see that it's getting anywhere and I don't like it."

Joan wasn't belligerent, but she was hurt. "I'm not a criminal, Mr. Gibson," she said.

Gibby grinned at her. "Millions of men in the armed forces have had theirs taken," he said. "They weren't criminals." He turned to Bannerman. "Did you kick up a fuss when the army took yours?" he asked.

"That was different," Bannerman answered.

"It was," Gibby agreed, "but not as different as you think. The army takes prints just in case they'll ever be needed for identification. We take prints for a variety of reasons. We need Miss Loomis' for identification. She spent three days in that apartment with your sister. She can't have been there all that time without leaving some prints around the place. Every inch of that apartment has been searched for prints. We find your sister's prints. We eliminate those. They are meaningless, normal expectancy since she lived in the place. We find the prints of her cleaning woman. Those can also be eliminated. She worked there. We have other prints and they can be equally meaningless. They will be if they happen to be Miss Loomis' because we know she was a visitor there. Beyond that we know of no one who could have been in there legitimately. We've already eliminated your sister's prints and those of her cleaning woman. If we can have Miss Loomis' to match up, we can eliminate hers. Then we'll know what residue we have to work on. In that residue can be the prints of all manner of people who left prints there legitimately but there may also be the prints of one person who should never have been there because, if he hadn't, your sister would be alive now."

Joan made an effort and got over looking hurt. Bannerman was less ready to relinquish his belligerence.

"That does sound reasonable," she said. "I did stay there and I did touch things and, even though it is none of my business, that woman Ellie had coming in to clean didn't clean too well. She could have been a lot more thorough from the look of the place. It's more than likely that my fingerprints are still on every last thing I touched over at Ellie's."

Bannerman was on the spot. Joan Loomis had seen the point. She was taking the completely reasonable view of it. He could hardly do less, but for some reason acquiescence was going against the grain. He still didn't like it. I wondered whether in some way or another he could have had some inkling of the fact that Gibby in his explanations had been far more reasonable than he had been candid, that it wasn't a question of a wide variety of prints out of which innocent ones had to be eliminated, that the truth of the matter was that there had been found in the apartment a fine collection of prints and that with the exception of the already eliminated prints left by the cleaning woman they had every last one of them been the prints of one single person. Asking for fingerprints in this case wasn't just the routine it usually is. This was special.

"I don't know what she'd want a cleaning woman for anyhow," Bannerman said. He had to find some channel down which he could run his annoyance since he had obviously lost the engagement over the girl's fingerprints. "She used to keep the whole house clean back home and that was a big house and stairs and everything. That little bit of a place, it wouldn't be anything for her to clean."

"Of course, it wouldn't," Joan agreed. "But you're forgetting, dear. Ellie couldn't do any of those things. She had to be very careful of her hands. If they got the least bit red or rough, that would be the end of her job."

Bannerman nodded. "It's crazy," he said. "It's all crazy—the way she lived, the way she died, her job, everything."

I was inclined to agree, but not so Gibby. Gibby's the sanguine type.

"It will make perfectly good sense before we're through," he said.

We had long since finished eating. We didn't have to take the girl all the way downtown for fingerprinting. We got it done over at Homicide West because that was much nearer. We also got some mug shots of her while we were at it and I think we got away with those only because Bannerman was waiting outside and he didn't know what we were doing.

The girl, so far as I could see, just didn't know anything. She took a wan sort of interest in the whole proceedings, but she asked no questions. I was about to say that I've never seen a woman with less curiosity, but actually I don't think that was precisely it. I had the feeling that she was as curious as anyone might have been under the circumstances but that she was suppressing it as she would suppress an impulse to sin. I could just see it. She was reminding herself that she was a good girl and good in the fullest sense of the word. This experience she was having was a brush with evil, and even as she went through it, she was holding herself inwardly aloof in an effort to come out of it unsullied.

We didn't keep her long and when we rejoined Bannerman he seemed to be holding his breath while his eyes ran over Joan Loomis in searching appraisal. Whatever it was he saw in that moment of probing examination of her person appeared to satisfy him. He relaxed. He even vouchsafed us something that was almost a smile.

Gibby told them that we wouldn't be needing them any more that night and he promised that we would be in touch with them as the investigation went forward. He asked them to hold themselves available, not to leave town before we gave them the word and, in the event that they moved out of the President Polk, to keep us apprised of their addresses.

Bannerman's almost-smile faded. He didn't seem happy about these instructions. The girl was out-and-out rebellious. She had had all of New York she wanted, all of that and far more. She was very sorry, but if Milton wanted to please her, they would be on the very next train that might be headed in the direction of River Forks.

"That's the way I feel myself," Bannerman said. "Anything you find out about what happened to Ellie you can write and tell us. I'm waiting here for only one thing."

"Let's not wait for anything, darling, please," the girl said.

"We'll have to wait," he said gently. "We'll have to wait till we can take Ellie home. You understand that."

She caught her lip between her teeth. "Of course," she murmured, and it was more a moan than a murmur. "But it can't take long to arrange that."

Bannerman turned back to us. "May I ask you to help me with the arrangements?" he said. "I don't know anything about undertakers here in New York and won't there be some papers I'll have to have?"

Gibby nodded curtly. "You'll have to have papers," he said. "We'll see that you get those and we'll help you with everything, but it's much too soon for any of that. It's no good trying to begin on that until we are ready to release the body."

That they didn't understand. Bannerman reminded us that he had said from the first that he wanted Ellie out of the morgue as quickly as possible. It was going to take him a long time to forget that she had been there at all, but he wasn't unreasonable. He realized that nobody could be blamed for that. It was most disagreeable but it was the place people did go to await identification, but now he had identified her. That finished it. He wanted her out of there. He wanted to take her home

138

where she belonged. He wanted to lay her to rest in the churchyard beside their parents.

Gibby was sympathetic but he was also firm. He was also way out in left field, but they didn't know it. He didn't actually say that the body had to remain in the morgue until we had established the identity of her killer and had apprehended that killer, but he did indicate as much. He said categorically that it could not be released until such time as we had no further need of it for evidence.

Even that made me nervous. Bannerman earlier that evening had threatened us with an "or else" and, on being asked, had explained that the "or else" meant he would get himself a lawyer. He didn't make that threat now but there was no guarantee that he wouldn't again come down with the idea and I didn't even want to think of what a lawyer might do with the way Gibby had been handling this pair.

Bannerman said nothing. He let it go at seeming baffled, frustrated, and wearily resigned. It was Joanie who kicked up the fuss, but I had the feeling that it wasn't quite the fuss she would have liked to make. She was treading lightly now. She insisted on nothing and she asked for nothing. She merely complained. This was a terrible city. It was a terrible thing for a girl to have to stay in such an awful place even for a day and there was no telling how many days it might still be. She was sorry for herself and she was sorry for Ellie. She made it quite clear that our great city was no fit place for the pure in heart, whether alive or dead.

Satisfied that whether they liked it or not, they knew what was expected of them and were ready to bow to his demands, Gibby turned them loose. We pulled out ourselves a couple of minutes later, taking with us Joanie's fingerprint record and some quick prints of her mug shots.

We headed downtown to the office. The various lab reports had been accumulating for us there. We went into a huddle with the fingerprint man. He set up the comparisons and we didn't have to wait for his expert opinion. There was no missing it. Those prints the boys had turned up so lavishly disposed about the apartment, the prints that had all been left by a single person and which, but for the already explained prints of the cleaning woman, were the only prints to be found anywhere in the place—those prints were the prints of Joan Loomis.

The set they had taken off the bathroom washstand was, as we had been told, perfect and complete. They were every bit as good as the set that had been taken from her for identification and you didn't have to be any sort of an expert to match those up. It did take some closer looking to determine that all the other prints, including the smudged ones and the partial ones, also matched, but our experts were definite on that and we could take their word for it.

I found myself looking back on Joanie's eagerness to be away from us and our city of evil and wondering whether she really thought it might be all that dangerous to the pure in heart or dangerous merely to a young woman who, on the evidence, had been in the wrong place at the wrongest of times and had, furthermore, lied to us about it.

The thing had begun to look open-and-shut to me. Sydney Bell, nee Ellie Bannerman, had been murdered in her bed. Some time after her death, her apartment had with the greatest thoroughness been wiped clean of all fingerprints and some time after that fingerprints had been sprinkled all over the place by Joan Loomis. I wasn't too astonished that Gibby was making no move to go straight up to the President Polk to place Joan Loomis under arrest. It wasn't quite as straightforward as all that, but in its own weird fashion it was straightforward enough to make me expect that we would be hightailing up there to subject the young woman to further questioning.

When you get a woman murdered that way in her own place and you have evidence that the place has been cleaned of all fingerprints, there is one inevitable conclusion to be drawn. The killer, afraid of having left a readable print, wipes everything to make certain and in so doing has eradicated all other prints along with his own. That makes sense. For Joan Loomis to have gone through that process and then later to have put her prints all over everything made no such ready sense.

It was like a message written on a freshly cleaned blackboard. It was emphatic and I was wondering what it could ever have been intended to tell us. Sifting it down in my mind, I found that it was telling me nothing beyond the fact that pure little Joanie had lied to us. I had not the first doubt that she had been in the apartment after Ellie Bannerman had been murdered and I was confronted with the inevitable question. Could Joan Loomis be the killer? She did have a corroborated alibi for the time of the killing. She had been in Boston with her cousin. That cleared her on that count, but even without her alibi, there was a second question that demanded answering. If she had been the killer, why would she wipe the place clean before she handled everything in sight and not after?

I asked Gibby that one. It gave him not a moment's pause.

"I wish it could be that easy," he said. "If that was the only thing that stood in the way of a clear picture of this thing, we'd be packed up and out of the ball park right now. Let's say she's the killer. She murders her future sister-in-law. She does everything she can think of to cover her traces, including the complete wipe-up of the place. She's ready to leave and she takes a last look around to make sure she hasn't forgotten anything. She spots something right out in plain sight. She'd thought she was being super-careful and here she's missed the obvious. She panics. She snatches it up, whatever it might have been, and then she goes all over the place again, looking everywhere just in case she's left something else that isn't in plain sight. She had been ready to leave. The ordeal of being in there with the body of the woman she had strangled had been over and now she's afraid to leave. She keeps searching and searching and her nerves grow more and more tense. Finally she is certain that she has looked everywhere. She is convinced that she has left nothing we can find and tie to her but she is in full panic and she tears out of there, forgetting completely that she should have re-peated the wipe-up. She has left us the most damaging evidence of all, and she has not only left it. She has pinpointed it for us. We have her fingerprints deposited on a blank page."

I don't say Gibby was giving me the full treatment on this. He wasn't painting the picture for me in quite as much vividly circumstantial detail as he would have put into it if I had been a jury, but he is one persuasive boy. He had me ready to write off the fingerprint deal as finished business. I dropped it to tackle him on the other loose ends.

"Then the next step is to determine how good her Boston alibi is," I said. "Crack that and we've got her."

Gibby nodded, but without enthusiasm. "We'll have Boston check it for us," he said. "They can question the cousin for what that might be worth."

"You sound as though you think the alibi is going to stand up," I said. "I don't see how it can unless her cousin will lie all the way for her."

"No," Gibby said. "It's going to check out for a Swiss cheese alibi. It will have holes well distributed through the substance. Remember that the chick found this wonderful bargain basement up there. Did the cousin shop with her or did she shop alone? If she shopped alone and was gone a full shopping day for it, that would be plenty long enough for her to have flown down here, done her job on this gal whose hands were her fortune and flown back again with a tale of all the bargains she'd seen."

"Seen and not bought?" I asked. "She could hardly have had time to do all her buying as well."

"She didn't have time to do all her buying," Gibby said. "She was at it all day today again. She hadn't wanted any New York merchandise. It was too sinfully expensive. That was the first tune she sang. It was a quick switch to the girlish bit about what fun it was to be foolish with money just once. If that babe was ever foolish with money it would have to have been confederate dough. Don't you see it? She comes back and tells her cousin that she's seen all manner of wonderful bargains but she hasn't bought any. She doesn't spend her money that way. She's going to sleep on it first and tomorrow she'll go back and buy what she decides she wants. She could have come back to her cousin's the day she flew to New York and she needn't have bought even a pin. The story would have been that it had been her research day and the next day she shopped. It would work but it did tighten her for shopping time."

"Tightened her enough," I agreed, "so that she had to finish her shopping today here in New York, despite the high prices."

"She's going to be Mrs. Bannerman and now she can afford it," Gibby said. "We don't begin to know what brother Milty will be inheriting beyond his sister's half of the house rent. Unless a will turns up somewhere that cuts him out, he'll inherit as next of kin and there could be considerable assets like bank accounts or brokerage accounts."

I sighed. "But at worst," I said, "there is half the house."

"At worst," Gibby agreed.

At this point we were interrupted. A detective came banging into the office to see us. It was a fellow named Harrity, Jim Harrity. We knew him well. I knew him because he had been transferred over to Homicide from Vice about a year back and we get to know all the cops who work Homicide. For Gibby it had been something like a reunion when Jim had come over from Vice. They had known each other way back. They had been at the Police Academy together.

Jim's a good detective, but he is also an inveterate comic. I could see right off that the antic mood was

144

upon him. He came in, confronted Gibby, and silently bowed low three times. Gibby yawned.

"The next time he gives you that angle, Mac," he said, "kick him in the pants."

"And stand charges for assaulting an officer?" Jim said. "You know better than that, oh, Master."

"What's the 'oh, Master' bit?" Gibby asked.

"Some people detect murders. You, oh, Master, read them in the stars."

"It's been overcast all evening," Gibby said.

"Tea leaves?" Jim asked. "Gypsy cards? The entrails of sacrificial birds? Crystal balls?"

"Balls to you," Gibby said. "If you've got anything, let me have it."

"It isn't much, oh, Master, but you didn't ask for much. One death by manual strangulation. This one's male."

"Who?" Gibby asked.

"You may not know him by name since you asked for him by motor vehicle registration number."

That brought me out of my chair. "Jerk," I exclaimed.

Jim looked plaintive. "Everybody calls me names," he said. "I get insulted at every turn."

"Spelled backwards," Gibby explained. "KREJ, Connecticut."

Jim shook his head. "Not that one," he said. "That's K. R. E. Jellicoe, scion of those Jellicoes whose genius was superior to their genes. The genius converted light metals into gold, much gold and most of it inherited by K. R. E., who is the marrying Jellicoe. At the moment he's got more millions than he's had wives, but he's a Jellicoe with all the Jellicoe efficiency and Jellicoe persistence and he's working at adjusting the balance. Give the boy time and the wives will top the millions. Have you ever seen him? He's built like a retired wrestler, two hundred and fifty pounds of moan and bustle."

For a moment I thought it was Jim who was clairvoyant because it wasn't too bad a description of Jellicoe as we had seen him on the table at Bellevue, when he was having the adhesive tape slapped on him; but then I remembered that Jim was an old hand at spoonerisms. I transposed it back to bone and muscle.

"We've seen him," Gibby said. "Twice and both times in trouble."

Jim was interested. "Murder kind of trouble?" he asked.

"Could be," Gibby said. "Meanwhile which one was killed?"

"Henry Camplin, also known as Henry Cameron, also known as Harry Cane. Less politely known as Harry the Pimp."

"Owner of the car I was checking on?"

"Registered to him," Jim said. "Owner of a nice little smelly record. When they switched me from Vice to Homicide I wondered how many of the old customers would move with me just because they were used to giving me their business. I was beginning to think I had no following at all, but things are looking up. Harry is the first."

"Procurer?"

"Was when I knew him last," Jim said. "I've checked with the boys over at my old shop. They say they haven't had a thing on him since I left and I remember on my own that there wasn't a thing on him for some time before that. It adds up to two years of retirement for

146

Harry or two years during which he's been smarter than us."

"Getting strangled is smart?" Gibby asked.

"The old brain can't be working all the time," Jim answered.

"Where did the body turn up?"

"His apartment. Two-roomer in the West Thirties. He had a broken window and he'd been yelling for the super to get a fresh pane of glass in it. The super didn't have any panes of glass. He had to buy one and he couldn't buy one without the authorization of the owner. That took time but he finally got it and he went up to put it in. He found the apartment door open and no answer to the bell, so he went in. He found Harry, warm as toast but dead as a herring."

"Been moved yet?" Gibby asked.

"Not yet. You can still see him *in situ*."

Gibby nodded. He reached for the phone and called Bellevue. He asked for the doc who had put K. R. E. Jellicoe on ice for us. He had to wait a bit while they located our boy. He was just checking on whether they still had him for us. They didn't have him. Within an hour after Jellicoe had gone up to the alcoholic ward his lawyer—and it was one of those legal names you conjure with—arrived on the scene with K. R. E.'s personal physician, also eminent. They'd had him out of there in what our spoonerizing friend, Jim, called three lakes of a sham's tail. Our Bellevue friend knew all about it. He'd been having a grim time over it. He asked only one thing of us. We were to go elsewhere for our favors thereafter.

Gibby didn't go after the grimy details. He had, after all, been cutting a corner on the thing and it hadn't worked out. If you want to be in a position to pull the big virtuous indignation act, you can't cut corners. It's nice to be able to wrap the law around yourself and take a firm stand. There wasn't any law Gibby could wrap around himself.

How it had been worked was obvious enough. The fact that neither Gibby nor I had recognized Jellicoe on sight didn't mean that anyone that rich and so much the darling of the tabloids would go unrecognized indefinitely. Some ward attendant or perhaps an ambulatory patient who could get to a telephone had come down with the idea our friend in Grand Central Station had laid before us. It could be a nice piece of change, Jellicoe's gratitude. K. R. E. asks this character to put a call through to his lawyer and tell the lawyer where he is and what's being done to him. After that it unfolds itself automatically. K. R. E., of course, wouldn't have had any piece of change on him just then but it could be worth obliging him just on the chance that he would remember later.

We pulled out of the office and headed for Harry's place. We had Jim Harrity with us. Gibby had a couple of chores for Jim to do. One was easy. He wanted a call put through to the President Polk to check on just what time Joan Loomis and Milton Bannerman had returned to the hotel and on whether they had remained there.

The other promised to be rather more difficult. He wanted to know whether our man in the brown hat was still waiting around Grand Central Station. The station police could have a look around for him but it had to be done on description alone. We had no name for him. Gibby worked at filling Jim in on the description.

I sat back and marveled, as I always marvel. This was no new thing with us. We see someone. It may be on the job and it may be just in passing. I get as good a look at this person as Gibby does. I have 20–20 vision and everything else it takes but I lack something that Gibby has. He has 20–20 attention. Whatever he sees he registers and what he registers he remembers. If you think that isn't remarkable, test yourself on it some time. Take somebody you see all the time. The waitress in your favorite restaurant will do. Sit down now and write out a description of her, every last thing you can remember. Put it in your pocket and the next time you go out to eat compare it with the original. You'll find out how little you observed, how little of that you remembered, and how little of that you had seen correctly. Any time you want to give Gibby the same test, you could take what he wrote down and use it to put out a wanted flyer and it would be as good as a mug shot.

Brown hat, medium height, solid build, ruddy skin— that would have been the total I could have come up with if I'd had to do it. Gibby knew that the man had brown, curly hair and gray eyes. He also knew that the man wore short sideburns, something between a normal cut and the full sideburn deal. He even knew that on the left side the man had a hairy mole just in front of his ear and he guessed that the purpose of the sideburns was to make it less conspicuous.

Harrity grinned. "Last time I saw that one," he said, "it was at Sing Sing. The prison barber doesn't go for sideburns. Skinheads are his style. That mole you talk about showed up as plain as plain."

"Also out of your old clientele?" Gibby asked.

"Harry the Pimp's nearest and dearest," Harrity answered. "Same line of work except with muscles."

I told myself that it had been too good to be true. We couldn't be getting all our identifications that easily. Brown hat was well built but he hadn't looked to be anything that would require special mention in the muscle line.

"He runs only average for beef," I said.

"That's the boy," Harrity insisted. "To look at him you'll assume he'll be easy to handle, but don't take any chances on it. I know him. He's all steel springs and cute. Mix it up with him and you'll find that they come no cuter. As long as I've known them, he's handled Harry's rough stuff for him. No matter how big they come, George cuts them down to size."

"George what?" Gibby asked.

"George Monroe," Harrity answered. "That's his right name, but he's also gone as George Madison, George Lincoln, George Adams, and George Johnson. He has a rare taste in aliases. It's always Presidents. One of these times he's going to be George Washington. I've been waiting for it."

"You know George and you know K. R. E. Jellicoe," Gibby began.

"Not exactly in the same way," Harrity interrupted to explain. "Over in Vice I used to get to arrest George now and again. K. R. E. was always the one who walked away from a raid and whose name was carefully omitted from the court proceedings."

"You've seen him though?"

"I've even tangled with him. There was one time when he was concerned for the lady's good name. He

150

thought he could wrestle long enough for her to get
some clothes on and get away. He didn't last the course.
He's big enough and strong enough but he's too clumsy
and too slow and too stupid."

"No match for George then?"

Harrity laughed. "Ever been to a bullfight?" he
asked.

"Yes."

"Then you know how much the bull outweighs the
matador and you also know which one usually gets cut
up and dragged out of the arena. Jellicoe's a bull and
he's not even a fighting bull."

"What about Mae?" Gibby asked.

"It comes after April and before June and it has
thirty-one days," Harrity said.

"Not it, she."

"Mae what?"

"Just Mae."

Harrity shook his head. "Leave us not switch roles,
oh, Master," he said. "You're the clairvoyant. I'm the
cop. Maybe I sounded brilliant on old George, the Presi-
dential range, but I wasn't picking him out of the whole
field. You gave me the mole and I was thinking along
the lines of Harry's associates. What does Mae look like?
She could have been calling herself June when I knew
her."

Gibby filled him in on Mae. That is, he filled Harrity
in as far as he had any filler to offer. This Mae was
known to Jellicoe, George, and Harry. She might or
might not have been giving a party to which George
and Harry might or might not have been taking Jellicoe.

We drew a blank on Mae. Harrity did run down for
us a list of dames given to party throwing, given to the

delusion that K. R. E. Jellicoe would be an ornament to one of their parties, and given to commissioning Harry or George or both to handle the issuing of invitations. None of these had he ever known as Mae. Any of them might be calling herself that at the moment.

"If you ask me, though," Harrity said, "I'm guessing that Mae will be a number I don't know. The boys have been out of trouble for a long time and it doesn't look as though they've been in retirement. The odds are they've been playing in some new backyard the Vice Squad has never caught up with yet. Mae is probably a new playmate."

"Or a new boss," Gibby suggested.

Harrity shrugged. "Who knows?" he said.

"Two years they've been smarter than you," Gibby told him. "They never were that smart before. Would you say they could have turned that smart all of a sudden?"

Harrity gave it the "oh, Master" routine again, but he conceded Gibby's point. If there was anything in the way of uncommonly effective thinking being done, it was being done for George and Harry, not by them.

We came to the house and Harrity dropped off to hit a phone and do the couple of chores Gibby had handed him. We went up to have a look at the new corpse.

six

This one was not only very new. It was also soaking wet. If it hadn't been for the fact that the marks of the strangler's hands were perfectly clear on the man's throat, I would have been prone to expect this one to be a death by drowning. Water was still streaming from the hair and drops of water stood on the dead man's skin. The body was completely naked. It lay across the threshold of the bathroom doorway and a large bathtowel lay in a heap on the floor beside it.

"Fresh out of the shower and reaching for his towel

when he got it," Gibby said. "Taken by surprise, I'd say."

The cops who were in there working the deal seemed to be seeing it the same way. I was coming down with a couple of reservations. I went back for a close look at the apartment's front door. There was no indication that there had been any tampering with the lock or forcing of the door.

"Killed by someone he left waiting while he went to take a shower?" I asked. "Or would it be someone who had a key to the place?"

"Could be someone who just walked in because the door had been left open," Gibby said.

The building superintendent was still hanging about, still clinging to the pane of glass he had been going to put into the window. He had a bit of information and he volunteered it.

"He was always doing that, Mr. Camp was," he said.

Gibby indicated the body. "That Mr. Camp?" he asked.

"Yes, him. He was always doing that, like I said. He wanted something done in here, like maybe put in a new washer or something, he'd tell me and he'd leave the door open so I could get in to do it. Off and on, it seems like, he had the door open more than it was shut."

"And he wanted the glass put in his window," Gibby said. "That makes it easy, doesn't it?"

"Trusting soul, extraordinarily trusting for his line of business," I remarked.

Gibby didn't see it that way. He argued that a procurer would ordinarily have no one to fear but the police and that locking the door to his apartment wouldn't do him much good if it was the police who wanted him.

"What about burglary?" I asked. "Most people in New York are at least a little bit concerned about the possibility of burglary."

Gibby swept the place with a quick glance. "What could a burglar get?" he asked.

From anyone it would have seemed a stupid question. From Gibby it seemed incredible. The answer couldn't have been more obvious. It lay right out in plain sight. When Harry had undressed for his shower he had draped his clothes over the back of a chair. He had taken off his watch and had left it lying on the table. It was a cinch that any money he would have had on him would have been in the pockets of his clothes. I pointed to the watch and spoke of the money.

Gibby conceded me a point, but he took the concession back almost as quickly as he had given it. It was quite true, he argued, that while Harry had been under the shower, someone could have slipped in and made off with his watch and his money. He even allowed that it was a nicer than average watch, a watch that a man might not care to lose. He went on to check the pockets of Harry's coat and pants. The pants pocket yielded something over a dollar in change. The coat pocket yielded a billfold and it was not too badly stocked. There was something over $150 worth of folding money in it. Gibby looked at it, counted it, and put it back. While he was at it, he went through the rest of the contents of the billfold. He didn't find anything much. There was a driver's license and there were about a half dozen little photographs. In the trade they call them art poses. The police have been bearing down on the places that sell them. Gibby showed more interest in them than he usually does in that sort of thing and, when he caught me looking at him quizzically, he explained.

"I just wanted to know whether Sydney Bell had posed for any of them," he said. "She was a model, you know."

It was an engaging idea. I took a good look. It didn't look like Bell and anyhow in these the photographer had most emphatically not been concentrating on hands.

"There are other models," I said.

"At the moment," Gibby said, "other models aren't much our business. We were talking about burglary. Here it is, available for a burglar: one good watch, something a little over $150 in cash, and six very high quality feelthy pictures."

"I've known burglars to show interest in a lot less," I said.

"A lot less," Gibby agreed. "But these would normally be on Harry's person. There isn't another thing in this place he would worry about losing. Since there's nothing around he worries about losing, he forms the habit of never giving burglars a thought. Comes the time when he doesn't have his valuables on his person, when he's under the shower, the old habit persists. He's careless. He doesn't give a thought to burglars."

"What about his clothes?" I asked.

"Also normally on his person any time he leaves the door open," Gibby said.

"Extra clothes?"

"I doubt that he has much," Gibby said.

He threw open the door of the one closet the place

158

had. There were a few things hanging in there, but they were little better than rags.

It was my first thought that here we had another one just like the first. Clothes are taken and money is left. I didn't speak the thought because Gibby had prefaced the opening of the closet with the remark that Harry hadn't owned much in the way of clothes. I asked about that.

"We've had one where only clothes seem to have been taken," I said. "It's screwy, but if it can happen that screwily once, why not again?"

Gibby pointed to the clothes hung over the chair. "Look at those," he said.

They looked all right to me, nothing like that worn junk that hung in the closet. Everything looked brand-new, in mint condition.

"He was a snappy dresser," I said.

"That he was," Gibby agreed. "New shirt, never been laundered. New shorts, never been laundered. Everything new. I know these snappy dressers. They own one suit at a time. If it needs a press, they sit in the back room of the tailor shop while it's being pressed. Cleaning, that gets done overnight. You check into a Turkish bath and by morning they've done the complete valeting job for you. Once in a while, maybe, you send something out to the laundry, but mostly when you need a clean shirt, you stop in and buy one, change into it in the store and don't bother to take the dirty shirt along."

"Sounds like an expensive way to manage," I said. "What's the purpose? No laundry marks for identification in case of trouble?"

Gibby shook his head. "No," he said. "It's usually a corpse who is identified by laundry marks and you don't often find one of these boys prone to look that far ahead."

I took objection to that. I remembered a killing we'd had down in the Village. It was one of the easier ones. The killer had bloodied his shirt in doing the killing. He changed out of the bloody shirt and left it while he took off in a shirt he'd swiped out of one of his victim's drawers. The laundry marks on the abandoned shirt had led straight to him. I reminded Gibby of that one.

He laughed it off. "What made that so easy," he said, "was that the dope had never thought of laundry marks. Anybody who'd thought of them enough so that he wouldn't want any wouldn't have left us the shirt."

I could hardly dispute that. I returned to my original question.

"Then why all this buying of new shirts instead of having the old ones laundered?"

Gibby shrugged. "A way of life," he said. "Sending laundry out is thinking ahead to next week when you are going to need a clean shirt. You're in a line of business where next week you'll just as likely as not be in jail, you live for today. It's particularly characteristic of these boys. Their arrest rate is high and their conviction rate is also high. Sentences, on the other hand, are short. A couple of months and they're back in circulation. Another couple of months and they're picked up again. It's in and out all the time for them, so while they're out they live from day to day. If you see much of them, you get so you can spot it. The day they're holding, they'll be the well-dressed man, everything the very latest wrinkle. Hit them when they've had a run of thin days and they don't look shabby. They look dirty. No clean shirt to change into and no dough for buying a clean shirt so they go on wearing it while the rim at the edge of the collar gets darker and darker."

While Gibby talked, he was going through all that fancy raiment the dead man had hung on the chair when he had gone to take his shower. He seemed to be looking for something and, whatever it was, he wasn't finding it. He talked to the cops who were working the place and told them to watch especially for any papers—receipts, storage checks. Anything of that nature they turned up he would be wanting.

Jim Harrity came bouncing in and interrupted him.

"They're all on the move," he said. "Maybe you can figure it."

"Bannerman and the girl gone from the hotel?" Gibby asked.

"They came in. They sat in the lobby together awhile and talked. Then they went up to their rooms. Then almost immediately they went out again, but fancy."

"How fancy?"

"He came right back down to the lobby and hung around. You know, trying to look like a potted palm. A minute or two later she came down and tore out to the street. He didn't join her. He followed her. The bellhops enjoyed the show. The way those hellbops have it, he was hanging around the lobby waiting for her to come down and go out. She did and he tailed her."

"That's two on the move," Gibby said. "What about George?"

"Full report," Harrity said. "The station cops know George and they know his record. He hangs around their station and gives a gal the eye, they watch him."

As Harrity repeated to us the full report, it became evident that the station cops had been keeping a good watch. They had given him the full deal on the part of it we had ourselves witnessed except that they did add an interesting detail even to that chunk of it. They had first spotted George when he had been watching the Incoming Trains bulletin board.

"Knowing the business he's always been in," Harrity said, "they naturally wondered if maybe he wasn't there to pick up a flesh shipment due in from the hinterland. Nothing much they could have done about it if he was, but you can't blame them for being curious."

"He was just watching the board?" Gibby asked. "Not trying to make any girl?"

"The girl came later. He had been there several minutes just watching the board when the girl turned up. She was watching the board, too, except that then George gave up on the board and took to watching her instead."

He went on from there to give us what we already had. The man who had come along behind the girl and put his hands over her eyes, the slap, the faint, the men from the DA's office who had talked to George, the whole continuity. Gibby hurried him through that part of it and asked him for anything they'd given him on George after that. They had given him plenty.

George had left the Incoming Train board and had sauntered over to a vantage point from where he could see through the glass doors into the waiting room. He had watched us until we had left the station, taking the girl and Bannerman with us. Then he had returned to his old place, but now he had been turned the other way, watching the ramp down to the suburban-trains level.

Periodically he had gone down to the lower level and waited at the gate of one of the Connecticut trains. He would wait there while the train loaded to go out and as soon as it had departed he would go back to his old post and watch the ramp again.

At this point Gibby had another question.

"This," he asked, "didn't happen until after we'd talked to him? He had shown no interest in the ramp or in the Connecticut trains before that?"

"Only in the Incoming board and the girl," Harrity said.

"Good," Gibby said. "He still in the station?"

"No, he's gone off with the girl."

At that point I had a question. This was going a bit fast for me.

"What girl?" I asked.

"Your girl," Harrity said. "The saint and flap dame."

"The what?" I yowled. Despite the hellbops of only a few moments before, I had completely forgotten about Harrity's spoonerisms.

"Faint and slap," Gibby growled. "Joan Loomis."

"I was guessing Joan Loomis," Harrity said smugly. "George was back watching the ramp. Your babe returned to the station and walked right up to George and engaged him in conversation. If it had been the other way around, maybe the station cops would have taken a hand, but the way it was they just watched. In fact, they had it figured that everything was under control because the girl talked to George and there was this guy who had followed her into the station. They knew him, too. He was the one who had soaked up the slap. He was right in there watching and they made the not-too-unnatural mistake of thinking he was one of your boys tailing her. So, when she left the station with George, and this man—he'll be Bannerman, of course—softshoed after them at a discreet distance, they told themselves it was all safely in the hands of the DA's office and they kept their own mitts off it."

Gibby sighed. "That leaves us only one," he said. "Jellicoe. What do they report on him?"

Harrity shook his head. "I exaggerated," he said. "I have nothing on Jellicoe. Nobody reports seeing him or anything that answers his description."

One of the lab boys who had been working the body had come over and was standing by waiting to talk to us. We took a break from Harrity and listened. What he had for us was one of those tiny fragments those boys so dearly love. It had come from under one of the dead man's fingernails. It wasn't of the order of those fine scrapings that sometimes yield up information under microscopic examination. This was big enough to be seen with the naked eye and enough bigger than that to be readily identifiable. It was a bit of colorless, transparent Scotch tape about an eighth of an inch wide and perhaps three-eighths of an inch long.

"It was hanging out from under his fingernail," the lab man said, "and it was quite dry. It isn't likely that he could have been under the shower with it without its washing away, but if it only washed loose, it wouldn't have been dry. It's a cinch he picked it up after he came out from under the shower."

Gibby gave it the works. He had every cop in town alerted to pick up on sight Milton Bannerman, Joan Loomis, K. R. E. Jellicoe, and the late Harry's friend, George. We already had the Connecticut police co-operating on a lookout for K. R. E., but Gibby wasn't satisfied.

"There's too much happening," he grumbled, "and we're not making enough of it happen. Too much of this is not under control."

"We're not making any of it happen," I interpolated hastily. "We don't even know that this second murder is connected with our case."

Actually I didn't want it connected. You have a murder investigation going and before you've even gone to first base with it, another murder pops at you. That isn't good. It's likely to draw some pretty serious criticism. There are always the wise boys who'll be ready to say that if the DA's office had gotten off its tail faster or acted more effectively, they could have held it down to only the one killing.

If this second strangling were to turn out to be linked to our first one, we'd be wide open to that sort of criticism, however unfair it might be. That was bad enough, but Gibby seemed to be wanting it worse than that. He seemed to be disgruntled over the fact that it hadn't been some move of ours that had precipitated the second killing.

"That much we do know," he insisted. "This one comes right out of the other one. It may only be a hunch but it's the best hunch we've got to ride."

"Look," I said. "We've been assigned to the Bell killing. Let's stay with that one. The Old Man can give this one to somebody else."

"What good is that?"

"Working on one at a time is enough. We don't have to be greedy."

"Don't be silly. The only person we've got really

165

linked to the Bell killing sneaks off to pick up with George, and George's buddy or partner or what have you turns up strangled. Where does the one case stop and the other start?"

"I don't know," I said. "But I think we ought to get to the Old Man, tell him what we know, and let him decide whether he wants us to work this killing or not. It is his office. Remember?"

"We haven't the time for that," Gibby said.

"What are we going to rush off and do now?" I asked.

I couldn't see that there was a thing we could do just then. It was clearly a matter of waiting till one or more of the people we wanted were turned up for us by the police. It wasn't that I didn't know Gibby well enough to realize that he would be itching to get out and look for them himself. It was rather that I couldn't see that there was any reasonable place we could go to start looking.

"Connecticut," Gibby said, answering me in a word.

It was a word I couldn't make much of.

"Jellicoe?" I asked.

"Jellicoe," Gibby said. "Harry here, according to his own story and to George's story, stowed Jellicoe's car away somewhere in a garage. He should have had on him a ticket for the car or a receipt or something. You were the one who was pushing the burglary angle and you may not have been too far wrong. I've been through all his pockets. No ticket, no receipt."

"So what do we do in Connecticut?" I asked.

"We see if Jellicoe's recovered his car and gone home. We have a talk with him."

"Now, look," I argued. "It's his car. There are lots of easier ways he could get it back. He wouldn't have to murder Harry for it. It's not as though there were any signs of a fracas. Harry was taken by surprise."

"Uhhuh," Gibby muttered noncommittally.

"Before we go hightailing off to Connecticut," I insisted, "we can call Jellicoe's doctor and lawyer. They pulled him out of Bellevue. He's probably with one or both of them right now."

"Okay," Gibby said. "You phone them. You just want to talk to him about his stolen car."

It was easy. I got on the phone and I made the calls. I got on to the lawyer first. He was much interested in the stolen car. He was more than interested. He was distressed about it. You may not know this big Wall Street attorney type, but we've tangled with them often enough to know them well. They're always dealing in millions, handling the affairs of people who own fleets of cars. You might think that this type would take the loss of one single car in his stride. It would be small stuff, but that isn't the way their minds work. It is property, client's property, and nothing is more important than client's property. He made no bones about it. Jellicoe's property losses were one of his major worries. K. R. E. was so careless. He didn't know what he was going to do about the boy.

I asked him where we could find the boy that night and he referred me to the doctor. He had left K. R. E. in the doctor's hands. I was just dialing the doctor's number when Gibby came over to the phone. He had a little card in his hand.

"No burglary," he said. "Here's the ticket for the jerk's little painted wagon."

"Where did you find it?" I asked.

"In one of Harry's shoes," Gibby answered. "He put

it there to keep it specially safe, but I don't know whether it was because he took his responsibility for the car so seriously or because he had made a couple of important notes on the back of it."

He turned the card so I could see the back. There were two names written on it. One was Milton Bannerman. The other was Joan Loomis.

I sighed. "All right," I said. "You win. This one does belong to us."

"How are you doing with their eminences?" Gibby asked.

"Just finished with the attorney. He's unhappy. The jerk is congenitally careless with his property and the fact that he can afford to be cuts no ice."

"He know where we can find his client?"

"He suggested I try the doctor. He left him in the doctor's care, but now that we have the receipt that angle's out."

"Murder's still in," Gibby said. "Let's try the doctor."

I dialed the number and got the doctor. He was easier to talk to than the attorney. He didn't have Jellicoe with him. He had seen him earlier in the evening, but he wouldn't have the first idea of where his patient might be now. I explained that we had seen him at Bellevue and had heard that he had left the hospital in the company of his attorney and his physician.

"That's right," the doc said. "If you want him badly, I'd suggest that you keep trying Bellevue. He should be turning up there again before the night is out."

"Bellevue?"

"He wasn't ready for the alcoholic ward when I saw him but he was on his way—on the way and eager. I had a time making him sit still even long enough for me to check over his dressings. Even when I told him that a Bellevue patch-up job is always adequate but that you can't expect a youngster who's working emergencies to be too much concerned over the possibility of leaving a few permanent facial scars, he was raring to go. I had to talk fast to get him to sit still long enough for me to take the dressings off and check them over. Actually he was all right. It was a nice clean job they did for him down there. The dressings were a little larger than necessary but all I did was fix him up with some fresh ones that looked a little less spectacular."

"Then you would guess that he didn't go on home after he left you?"

"Any place but home. I've known the boy all his life. He graduated to me out of the hands of his pediatrician. He was full of steam while I was working on him. That fight he was in must have interrupted his drinking and he was in a full spate of eagerness to go back and get on with it again."

"The fight?" I asked.

"No, the drinking. He'll be ready for the alcoholic ward before morning."

It was evident that the man wasn't quite as much resigned as he tried to sound. He did go into considerable detail in his explanation of the efforts he had made to quiet the jerk down. He had tried to give him a sedative, offering it on the ground that changing the dressings was going to hurt, but Jellicoe had fought off both needle and tablet. The night had been young and the jerk had been raring to go.

I hung up and gave Gibby a full report on the conversation. So far as I could see, Gibby was in something of the same frame of mind as the doctor had just been describing to me in his discussion of K. R. E. Jellicoe. Gibby was also raring to go and there wasn't going to be anything to dampen him down. He did give me an attentive hearing, but it seemed to me that he was enjoying this intelligence I'd had from Jellicoe's physician far more than its content warranted. He appeared to be finding it quite as stimulating as he had found the notes written on the back of the garage receipt.

"This adds up," he said, when I had finished. "It adds up to the craziest sort of totals, but it does add up. I've had a check on where the jerk lives in Connecticut and I've been looking at the timetable. He lives in Westport and a train was leaving for Westport right at the time we were fixing it up with Bannerman to pull the guess-who routine on his girl friend. The station cops tell us that George didn't start keeping an eye on any New England trains till after we'd had our talk with him and now we have exactly the same thing on our own observation. You have to hand it to George. He had all the answers for us. He thinks on his feet."

"The way I add it," I said, "all this means he was in the station because of Joan Loomis and not because of Jellicoe. That's what every bit of evidence is screaming at us, isn't it?"

"Unless," Gibby said, "he was there because of Joan and Jellicoe."

"How do you make that?" I asked.

"Bannerman's dames," Gibby said. "It could be that his sister looked worse than she was. It could also be that he's been working overtime at making her look better than she was. It can be the same way with his girl friend. Is Joan as good as she seems? Was it drink the jerk was thirsting for while his doctor changed his dressings? He does have a reputation for hitting the bottle, but he has an even noisier reputation for having a thing for the dames. The first time we noticed him he was buying a red nightgown. Does he want a nightgown of that kind if all he has on his mind is liquor? I haven't known him all his life, but I can make a better guess than his doctor did at what it was he was so eager for. Add it up. He wanted it. George is in the business of providing it. How would it add up if Joan should be what George is providing tonight?"

I shrugged it off. "We can't do anything about that till we find them," I said.

"We can look for them. That's why we're heading for Westport right now."

"You have the car receipt. That means the car is still in the garage and the station cops don't say that George and Joan headed for any Westport train. They left the station."

Gibby nodded. "And if George knew where Harry put the car," he said, "there might be no need of the receipt. Jellicoe could go around to the place, identify himself, and take it out without a receipt."

"Easy enough to find out if he did," I said. "We call the garage and ask."

Gibby laughed. "I've already had one of the boys do that," he said. "I wasn't telling you because I thought I could cut down the arguments. The car's still there. Nobody's come around for it."

"So," I said, "why Westport?"

"Because it's a place to look and we have no other place. The car is no obstacle. They could have gone up there in Harry's car. Last we saw of that one, George was driving Jellicoe away in it. As far as we know, it's been available all along. Not to speak of George. What's to say he doesn't have a car of his own?"

We left Harry and his apartment to the Medical Examiner's men and the cops. We went down to the car and headed out for Westport. I can't say that I went kicking and screaming. I just went. Nothing Gibby had said made it seem anything but the most futile of errands; but, as I saw it, Gibby did want to be on the move and there would be no holding him down. This seemed to be as good a move as any. It would give the boy something to do until the police came through with one or more of the people we wanted to talk with. If he was going to go off half-cocked on any harebrained enterprise, it seemed a good notion to let him blow off his steam by driving out the Merritt Parkway. That was safe. He could easily have come up with some far more hazardous idea.

By the time we started up there, it was late enough so that we didn't have any traffic to hold us down, but even at that it was a longish drive. First you have to get yourself out of the city and then you're crossing the full width of the broad suburban encirclement. You're well out the far side of that before you hit Westport. That much driving takes time even when you know where you're going, but for us Westport was only the beginning. We still had the Jellicoe place to find and precious little open that time of night where we could ask.

We made a try at an all-night gas station, but the sleepy attendant was new to the neighborhood. He wasn't so new that he didn't know the Jellicoe reputation—his knowingly salacious smirk covered that—but

172

he was too new to be any help to us. It was somewhere out one of the back roads. That was as close as he could come to telling us.

"Them millionaire places," he said, "they're all out back roads with the woods grown up around them so you'll think maybe they're farms been let run down or like that. In back of the woods and all that stuff they got the houses and the swimming pools and all. It's so they can have them orgies and nobody sees and nobody hears. That's the way it is when you're holding, but you got to hold the way they hold. You can't do it with no peanuts."

We made our second try at a lunchroom. There were two guys in there and they both knew exactly where the place was and they both told us, simultaneously. One had us turning left at the second crossroads. The other had us turning right at the third fork. When we left them, the third-fork man was offering to bet the second-crossroads guy five bucks that he didn't even know which way was up. Purely on our own intuition, or to be more precise about it, on Gibby's, we found our way around to the local State Police barracks. They did know the way and they showed it to us on a map. They said they didn't have a man out there, since the local constabulary was on it, but they'd had a report from the locals. Jellicoe hadn't come home and the place was deserted. All the servants had quit the week before and there hadn't been any replacements.

"He been up here without servants?" Gibby asked.

"That's what they tell me, though the story is that he's got to have somebody to wipe his nose for him even."

Following the road instructions, we crossed through

173

the town and turned off the highway into a tangle of woods roads. I was guessing that they would have been beautiful by daylight—trees and curves and all the wild nature any man could ask for. By night, and it was one of those dark, overcast nights, it was as black as the inside of my pants pocket, but airier. To a city boy's nose that air was something special. It smelled woodsy and it would have been quieter than the grave out there if it hadn't been for the crickets.

"I understand they make that noise by rubbing their legs together," I said.

"They should have them honed to a fine edge by now," Gibby muttered. "I wish they'd quit. They make me jumpy."

"They make other crickets jumpy too. To a cricket that's a very sexy sound."

"Yeah," Gibby said. "This is sexy country out here."

Taking the last of a complicated series of forks, he rolled into a road that was different from the ones we'd been traveling. It was narrower, but it was better paved. It was, in fact, impeccably surfaced. It was also by many a turn more tortuous than even the curviest job we had encountered up to that time.

"Private road?" I asked.

"Right," Gibby said. "We're now on Jellicoe property."

We continued on Jellicoe property for a good five minutes.

"There's a lot of it," I said.

"There has to be a lot of it," Gibby said, "to provide enough screen for the orgies."

"They had better be a pretty sober sort of orgies," I

muttered, "or people will be killing themselves all over this road."

This Jellicoe place didn't have the look of any run-down farm. It was more like a bit of the primeval wilderness that even the most assiduous of early New Englanders might have passed up as untillable. The trees that loomed by the roadside were rough-barked, thick-boled jobs that represented centuries of growing. Where there weren't these trees there was a ravine instead and the ground dropped sharply away from the road shoulder down to the rocky bed of a running brook. We could hear its babble as we drove along and when Gibby switched on the car searchlight and turned it that way, we could see the rocks and the way the water broke around them. An uncommonly pretty place; at this moment it was also grim.

The road ran along the rim of the ravine for a considerable distance and then it doubled around again and the big trees again enclosed it on both sides. I had expected that when it broke out of all this heavily wooded land, if it ever did break out, we would come on some broad expanse of lawns and some great, imposing house. It wasn't like that at all. We did abruptly come out into the open but it was no broad expanse. It was instead what seemed only an intimate bit of garden with a smallish house set at the far end of it. There was a car parked by the house and a man detached himself from the car and came toward us. Gibby slowed down, following the road through the garden, and I realized that the space was actually larger than it seemed and I guessed that the house also would be larger than it looked.

The man called to us. "Mr. Jellicoe?" he said.

"New York County DA's office," Gibby answered.

We stopped and the man came and leaned against the car window.

"You're the ones asked us to keep an eye out for Jellicoe," he said. "What's the trouble now? Drunken driving again?"

"That could be a part of it," Gibby answered.

"You're not kidding," the man said.

This, I knew, would be the local constabulary. He was of youngish middle-age, a bit balding, a bit fat. He wasn't the sort of police officer that impresses anyone with the dignity of the law or with its majesty, implacability, or fearsomeness. This man represented a more kindly, a more flexible, a more understanding law. It was a law that had had long experience of the weaknesses and foibles of mankind, a law that knew more about folly than it did about anything really evil. I could well imagine this officer being quite as firm as might on any occasion be necessary, but he would be gently firm. In speaking of Jellicoe he was taking a tone that was compounded of about equal parts of fatherly mildness and grudging admiration. I could guess that he didn't too much mind any Jellicoe escapades. He might even welcome them as further embellishments to a local legend.

We got out of the car and looked around. The house was completely dark and completely empty. The officer assured us of that. He had been in it.

"Find an open window?" Gibby asked.

"Just about everything's open," the man answered.

He went on to explain that this part of it was nothing new in the legend. It happened periodically. Jellicoe drank pretty much all the time, but periodically there would be one of these crescendos in his drinking and he would reach a pitch where he was too difficult to live with. At that point whatever servants he might have would quit him and he would go on in the house alone. That would last only a day or two and then he would leave it, go off somewhere, be gone a matter of weeks.

Some time during his absence, his long-suffering attorney would come up to the house, survey the damage, restaff the place, and see to necessary repairs. Eventually Jellicoe would return, sober and chastened, but after a few weeks of that, the drinking would start building up again and it would all be to do over again. His departures, therefore, were always highly disorganized forays and he couldn't be expected to shut windows or lock doors behind him.

"The garage is locked," the officer volunteered. "He always remembers that. Furniture, stuff in the house, he doesn't give a hoot, but he does care about his cars. He cares when they're in the garage anyway. Out on the road the way he is you'd think you could buy them in the dime store. He runs them into trees. He dumps them in ditches, but that's just his drunken driving, of course."

"Uhhuh," Gibby said. "He's careless with his other possessions, but he's merely incompetent with his cars. How many has he?"

"Three. A sedan, a convertible, and a station wagon."

We took a look through the house. As the officer had indicated, it didn't take any doing. We just walked in by the unlocked front door. Immediately we were inside the place we were crunching broken glass under our shoes. For Jellicoe to have reduced the place to that state of wreckage in just a day or two made him a wrecker of impressive capacities. Chairs and tables were overturned. It was obvious that he had been opening bottles by smashing their necks against the stonework of the fireplace. I suspected that at some point he might have been swinging apelike from the window draperies since only the rags of them remained and those were hanging askew.

"He do this all by himself?" I asked.

"He always does. One time I remember he went right through the place and kicked the glass out of every window. It takes him like that."

"It was just as well he was alone when he got in this mood," I remarked.

The officer reminisced about the first time he had ever seen one of these Jellicoe wrecking jobs. He had assumed that it couldn't just be this simple destruction. He had felt certain that it must have been a fight and he had gone through the whole house looking for blood.

"Matter of fact," he said, "I was even looking for him. I was sure I'd find him somewhere here and murdered at least. He wasn't. No blood, no body. I know him better now. He doesn't do this if there's anyone around. This is only when he gets lonesome. It's the one thing he hates worse than anything, being alone."

We left the house and went around to look at the garage. It was quite as reported, tightly locked up. The house was more interesting and we were headed back to it when the crickets stopped shrilling. Maybe they didn't really stop. I don't know whether noises bother crickets or not. Anyhow if they were still shrilling, we couldn't hear them. They were drowned out. From the woods came a spine-tingling squeal. It took me a moment to identify it for what it was and by that time

Gibby was off on the run. It had startled us, but it hadn't been anything really frightening, just a screaming of brakes, the sort of sound that comes just before the crash of a bad traffic accident or before that sickening silence of the accident most narrowly averted.

I followed after Gibby, and the officer pounded along beside me. Gibby already had the car started by the time we reached him and we just managed to hurl ourselves into it before he picked up speed. We zipped around the driveway that circled the garden and plunged into the woods. We were just into that blackest part among the trees when we heard the crash. This one, I was thinking, wasn't the accident narrowly averted. It was the accident.

It was only a matter of moments before we were out to the place where the trees dropped away on one side of the road and we were skirting the ravine. Then we saw it: the torn underbrush at the roadside. Gibby pulled up and we looked down over the edge. There was a car down there. It lay overturned among the rocks.

We jumped for the road and scrambled down to the wrecked car. This time it was the local officer who was in the lead. Gibby had to get out from behind the wheel and I had been riding wedged between them. Gibby and I were still on the way down when the cop reached the bottom and disappeared behind the car. We were going to have to work from that side if we were to get the driver out of that wreck.

I was still scrambling down the bank when Gibby hit the stream bottom. There was no footing to speak of and I was going down with my face to the bank, making use of every bit of rock outcropping for either a foothold or a handhold. I turned my head to try to see because I wanted to estimate whether I was far enough down to make the rest of the distance with a jump. What I saw made me forget the distance. I jumped.

Gibby was just started around the back of the wreck, going the way the officer had gone. I didn't see an arm or even a hand. I just saw the rock, a big hunk of it, hover a moment over his head and then crash into his skull. I saw Gibby go down and I made the leap, landing right beside him. He was lying in the water. I could feel it just above my shoe tops and I was thinking that even though that would be only inches deep, a man could drown in as little as an inch of water if he was unconscious and lying face down in it. I bent to help Gibby. That was the first thing to do, flip him over on his back to make sure he wouldn't drown. I was bending to him when the hands came around my throat. They fastened there and squeezed. I struggled. I know I struggled but even now I can't remember it as something I was doing. I had this feeling that I was separated from my body, standing away from it somehow and that the arms and legs I had flailing about, although they were mine and I could feel them, didn't really belong to me. Gradually I felt them less and less and after a bit I felt nothing, not even the sharp chill of the water in which I lay.

seven

It was pain that brought me back and, as I remember it, I came back just as I had gone out. Again I was struggling and again there was that feeling of separation from my body, from all the violent movements of my arms and legs. Gradually, however, I did become more clearly aware of myself. I was struggling to free myself from the clasp of those powerful hands around my throat and then quite suddenly I realized that I had nothing against which to struggle. I was free. The hands were gone and only the pain of them remained. It took some more time—and it could have been seconds or it could have been hours since I was in that state where everything seemed agonizingly slowed down, the state in which a man can be sharply aware that he is blinking his eye but with a peculiar sort of slow-motion awareness in which the lids seem to be creeping together and then creeping apart again.

I shan't even try to estimate how long I was in the process of realizing that there was more to the pain than what the strangling had done to me. I was coughing; and coughing, when your throat is that bruised and sore, is an acutely painful business.

I had quite forgotten Gibby and I had quite forgotten where we were. After a while he groaned and he tried to sit up. He didn't make it on that first try, but he did pull up far enough to take his weight off my shoulder. I found that I could sit up and I helped him. We sat together right in the middle of that little stream. It didn't matter. We were both of us as wet as we ever could be and it seemed unimportant.

"Mac," Gibby said feebly. "It is you, Mac?"

I tried to answer him and I was astonished by the sound I made. It was an odd, little croaking whisper that bore no relation to any words I'd planned to speak. I didn't, in fact, think I was making the sound at all until I'd tried again. That second effort wasn't any more of a success but I found it so sharply painful that I could make no mistake about one thing. That sound, however odd it was, was being ripped out of my own throat.

"The cop," Gibby muttered. "Where's the cop?"

His voice was a little stronger and steadier but the rest of him wasn't. He was trying to get to his feet and he flopped about as though he were made of soft rubber. I took him by the shoulders and I sat him down again. I was coughing like a fool. My eyes smarted and the tears kept running out of them. It wasn't the pain of the coughing that was making me cry, however, even though that coughing did hurt. It hurt even more than did my abortive efforts at trying to speak. The tears, nevertheless, were a completely separate thing. They were caused by the smarting of my eyes. It wasn't the other way about. I did figure that out for myself and I remember that it made me feel much better. I was alive again. I knew what was going on. It may not sound like much to you but I can remember that I took it big.

I went to look for the cop. In the standing up and moving around department I wasn't anything too great myself, not there at first, but there was the overturned car to hang on to and by holding on with both hands I did manage it. I got around to the other side of the car and by then stuff was coming back fast. I remembered that I had a flashlight and I even remembered to pray that the wet hadn't shorted it. I brought it out of my pocket and tried the switch. It hadn't shorted.

So then it fell right out of my hand and landed in the stream. That was a good light. Even the full submersion treatment didn't do it in. I could see the glow of it under the water and when I reached down and fished it out, it was dripping but the light held steady. What it lighted made me want to vomit but I made myself not think about that. I couldn't have vomited then, no matter how much I wanted to. My throat was hurting too badly.

The light fell on the body of that country cop who had made it down into the ravine ahead of us. I dropped down beside him and felt for breathing and heartbeat but I knew it wasn't going to be any good. He was lying there with his head bashed in and I was remembering the rock I had seen come down on Gibby's head. I saw right off how dead this one was and there was nothing for it but that I work my way back to Gibby as quickly as I could. Don't ask me how, wet as I was, I could know I was sweating, but I did know. It was a part of knowing the rest of it, of knowing that it had been the same rock that had reduced this man's head to a mash of hair and blood and skull splinter and brain. This one was dead and I had to hurry back to Gibby because I couldn't believe anything except that he would necessarily be dying. It had been the same rock.

I rammed the flashlight back into my pocket and worked my way back to the place where I had left Gibby sitting. I brought the light out again and turned it on him. He gave me a feeble grin.

"I suppose your cigarettes are as wet as mine," he said.

I felt for my cigarettes. Now that he had spoken of them I wanted one worse than I had ever wanted anything before in my life. I wasn't even thinking that I could hardly have endured smoking then, the way my throat was feeling. The pack was a sodden mess. I threw it away.

"Soaked," I said.

It was hoarse and it wasn't more than a whisper and it did hurt getting it out, but I was speaking again and that should have made me feel better. I don't think it did. What did make me feel better was Gibby. He was coughing as much as I was except that his sounded more like normal coughing. There wasn't any of that hoarse croaking in it. I brought the light out and had a good look at his head.

It was bloody enough. One ear was ripped and blood crusted and above the ear he was a mess of hair and blood all matted up together, but his head looked to be the right shape and that was encouraging. That cop's head wasn't anywhere near being the right shape any more.

"Find the cop?" he asked.

I didn't answer. At that moment my worry was for the living.

"Do you know what happened to you?" I asked.

"Whatever it was," he said wryly, "I guess it's all right because I seem to have survived it. Did that cop go off and leave us here to get our pants wet?"

"You were slugged with a rock," I told him. "Luckily it didn't hit you squarely. One of your ears looks half ripped off and maybe you have a little hole in your head but you look as though you could be repaired. The cop's beyond repairing. It wasn't any glancing blow he ran into."

"Dead?"

"Head smashed in, but completely. He's dead."

"Driver of the car?"

"Look," I said. "Somebody killed the cop. Somebody made a good try at killing you with the same rock. Somebody barely missed out on strangling me to death. There wasn't anyone around but the driver of the car and you weren't expecting him to hang around here mourning us."

"Is that what's wrong with your voice?" Gibby asked.

"Part of what's wrong," I said. "This coughing isn't helping it any."

"Then stop coughing."

"You're coughing as much as I am."

"It's because something's burning around here somewhere. The smoke is drifting down into this gully."

"What I can't understand is why he didn't kill me," I said. "He killed the cop."

Gibby grinned at me again. "What about me?" he asked. "Don't I count?"

"He thought he had killed you. He slugged you the same way he had slugged the cop and you dropped face-down in the water. You were out cold and a cinch to drown."

"And I didn't drown," Gibby said. "I see what you mean. I'm alive because you were under me. I was lying on your shoulder and that lifted me enough to hold my face out of the water. He slugs me and drops me. That takes care of me. I'm drowning. Then he gets his hands around your neck and strangles you. He strangles you just enough to put you out and then he lays you carefully in the stream with your head enough out of water so you won't drown and props me on top of you so I won't drown either. It doesn't make sense. Nobody's that inconsistent."

"To hell with him," I said. "We're alive and it's no thanks to him. What we need now is a doctor."

"First one that comes swimming down this brook," Gibby said, "I'll flag him."

I had a better idea. "I think I can make it up to the house," I said. "I'll telephone from there and get us help."

"I'm getting tired of the sitzbath," Gibby said. "We'll both try to make it."

I wasn't sure that was a good idea. "Do you think you should even try to move?" I said. "You could have some fracture."

"I don't feel fractured." Gibby made another try at standing and this time he made it. "I'm coming back fast," he said. "I've even figured out why he didn't kill you. He thought he'd killed you but when he quit on you, you were only blacking out and you had enough left to prop me against your shoulder and save me before you finally did black out."

"So I'm a hero," I said. "Do we both have to be heroes all in one night? Can't you take it easy now till I get a doctor to look at you?"

"I feel fine now," Gibby answered. "Nothing like a cold dip to put the zip back in a man. Don't you want to know how he managed to miss killing you?"

"I'm not uninterested," I said.

"The answer's cute," Gibby said. "He's had no experience with victims who have their clothes on. When it was the Bell-Bannerman girl, he worked on her naked throat and it was the same with Harry. With you he put on the same pressure for quite as long a time but he wasn't taking into account your collar and necktie. They made the difference. He thought he was squeezing hard enough because it had been plenty hard enough for the others but it was just not hard enough for an insulated throat."

"It was plenty hard enough to suit me," I said.

"Sure," said Gibby. "Let's have a look at the cop."

"He's dead," I protested. "Also he's across the state

line. This is Connecticut and we don't have the first bit of jurisdiction. We can't do a thing for him and a doctor could do a lot for us."

"What'll a doctor do? Give us cough drops maybe?"

He was hanging on to the car and working his way around to the side where I'd found the body. I went along after him. I'd come back enough so that I could have done it no hands if the footing hadn't been so bad. I was managing very well holding on with only one hand. I had the other for the light.

Gibby came on the dead cop. I held the light while he examined the body. I saw his hand go to the side of his own head. He is human, after all, and I'll defy anyone to take a crack in the head and then look at what he was looking at and not have that reflex that would make him put a hand up to check on whether his was the way it ought to be, with the hair on the outside and the brain on the inside.

He didn't say a word but, reaching for my hand, he moved the beam of the light so that it shone up into the overturned car. The car had hurtled over and landed with its hood propped up against the far bank. The hard top had held. It was somewhat bent but it hadn't crushed in appreciably. One door hung open and half torn from its hinges.

"He had just gotten out and was about to go away from here when we came down on him," I said. "A man can have an accident. Why was he so bent on killing the three of us?"

"Back door," Gibby muttered. "Why would he get out by the back door? That would be doing it the hard way." He moved my hand some more so that the light

190

shone right into the driver's seat. "No," he said. "He never got out."

I didn't have to ask him how he knew. I was seeing it for myself. It lay in a huddle against the locked door and it was all too obviously dead. Gibby took the light out of my hand and wormed his way far enough in the open door to lean over and make a close examination. He shone the light full on the face and it was a face we knew. It was Jellicoe's self-appointed guardian. It was the redoubtable George who had liked to call himself after Presidents. When Gibby held the light close, my hand went to my throat just as his earlier had gone to his head. I'm human too. I could see the purpling marks of strangulation on the man's throat just above his collar and in the very same place at the edge of my own collar I could feel the welts of just such marks.

"Then it wasn't an accident?" I said.

"It wasn't an accident," Gibby said. "George had someone in the car with him and he made the mistake of letting that someone ride behind him. That someone reached forward, got a good grip on George's throat and strangled George. Remember how we heard the squeal of brakes and then some time later we heard the crash? George struggled under the strangler's hands but he managed to stop the car. The strangler hung on till George went limp. Then the strangler opened the back door, perfectly natural for someone in the back of the car, and got out. The car didn't run over the edge into this ravine. It was pushed over with George in it and the strangler came down after it to make sure George was finished. There's one funny thing about it. Just a little bit of quite incidental accident, Mac, but that bit of accident saved your life and gave you the chance to save mine."

"What accident?" I asked.

Gibby told me. George's head had that oddly twisted look that heads just can't have unless the neck has been broken. The killer had strangled George and had come down after him to make certain he was dead. The killer had found George quite dead but hadn't known that in the overturning of the car George's neck had been broken. Gibby was betting that the actual cause of death was the broken neck. Legally nothing could have mattered less since the broken neck was the result of the tumble into the stream bed and that was the result of the strangling and of the killer's pushing the car over the edge. As Gibby was seeing it, however, the killer knew nothing of broken necks. The killer had found George dead, had assumed that he'd died of strangulation and had therefore not learned that more pressure would be needed to do the job on a man who was wearing collar and necktie. I was the lucky man. The killer had still not learned that when my turn had come.

"Last seen leaving Grand Central Station in the company of Joan Loomis," I said.

"Followed by Milton Bannerman," Gibby added. "Our girl is still knocking them dead. We'd better go up to the house and do some telephoning."

I haven't the first idea of how long it took us. It wasn't that it was so long a way to go or that, except for the first scramble up out of that gully, it was anything but the easiest sort of going. It was rather that we weren't up to much. On that little climb up to the road I had to give Gibby a hand, and when we reached the top he was completely done in. He had to flop in the grass and rest awhile. I kept telling myself that I should leave him there resting and go on to the house myself, but I couldn't whip myself up to the point of actually doing it. I needed some rest myself.

We lay there for a few minutes, and when Gibby asked me for my light, I thought for a moment that the old boy was looking for an excuse to prolong the rest period. I handed over the light but I was thinking that he needed no excuses for me. I was happy enough to postpone indefinitely the agony of making any further effort. A brisk little wind had come up and I found myself shivering in my wet clothes. I could feel Gibby beside me. He was shivering, too, and I marveled at the fact that we had both stopped coughing. It did seem as though cold should have made our coughing worse but the smoke was gone and that helped.

"We're right about how George died," Gibby said.

He was playing the light on the road. I didn't have to ask any questions. I'd already had the theory from Gibby. Now we had the evidence to back up the theory. The skid marks were as plain as they could be. You could see just where the tires had bitten against the road. It would have been at the time when we heard the squealing of the brakes that they would have been doing that, and, just as there had been a gap of time between the brake squeal and the crash, there was a corresponding gap of space to be seen on the road surface. George had brought the car to that screaming stop, but he had kept it squarely on the road. There was a good three feet of space between the end of the skid marks and the road rim, where the gully lay beyond.

Gibby couldn't have had it more exactly. The car had been pushed to the road edge and pushed over the edge to crash in the stream bed below.

Gibby got to his feet and stood over me, swaying. If he could make it, I had to try. I made it more easily than I'd expected and I didn't sway. We headed for the house. We'd go a bit of the way and then we'd rest again, but bit by bit we did make it. Gibby fell into a chair and let me do the telephoning. I called the locals and while I was at it I also called the State Police. I thought I knew what I was telling them but I won't take any oaths on it. Among other things, I knew that I had asked one or the other to bring a doctor along and after I'd finished on the phone and Gibby insisted that I'd pulled the doctor bit on both sets of police, I didn't believe him. I still don't know whether I did or I didn't. In any event, we did get two doctors. It wasn't too many. The spare one looked me over while the other worked on Gibby. I didn't need anything but checking and a slug of the brandy the doc had in his bag. The brandy was painful in my throat but it was worth the pain.

The boy that was working on Gibby had rather more to do. He had stitches to take in the scalp and a couple more to take in the torn ear. Gibby did better than I had in the brandy department. He didn't have a sore throat.

Both doctors were of the opinion that we should be taken to the local hospital and tucked into bed so we could be watched. I found the idea more than a little seductive, but Gibby would have none of it. Since they were more concerned about his condition than they were about mine, they took his refusal as going for the two of us and I was stuck with it.

By the time the medics had finished with us, the whole mass of cops was milling around and swapping ideas on how they could handle a matter of a stolen car when they had no way of knowing which car had been stolen or even if any had been stolen. My first guess was that they were talking about the car in the gully and I thought that they were being excruciatingly irrelevant and blatantly idiotic. I was about to tell them as much when Gibby spoke up.

"You've looked at the garage?" he asked.

They had looked at the garage. They reported that the doors had been broken open and that there was only one car in there, a station wagon.

"How many would there be if it was full?" Gibby asked.

"Three."

"Station wagon," Gibby said, ticking them off, "a bronze Cadillac and what?"

"Another Caddy. Red and chromium sedan. People keep mistaking it for a fire engine."

"The bronze job's in a New York garage," Gibby said.

We went around to have a fresh look at Jellicoe's garage. The doors were standing open now and it took no great feat of sleuthing to spot the damage to the lock. It had been hit a smashing blow that had knocked it completely askew. The heavy tongue of the lock didn't come within inches of meeting the socket. It had been driven downward from the horizontal to an angle of about forty-five degrees.

Gibby did a thorough job of examining the smashed lock and the splintered wood of that part of the door which was just below the lock tongue, and then he suggested to the cops that it could do no harm if they were to put out a stolen car alarm for the red and chromium job. They could get all the registration material on it out of their records. It was worth doing just on the chance.

"What about the car down in the brook?" he asked. "It has New York plates. I didn't get the number."

I hadn't even noticed that it had New York plates, much less thinking that I should have looked for the number. They gave Gibby the number and we went back to the house so he could phone New York and have our boys look that one up. He came away from the phone full of the old stuff. There was nothing more for us to do in Westport. We were driving back to town.

"Who's driving?" I asked.

"You are," Gibby said blithely. "I have moments of double vision. Every time I get cracked on the head, I come down with it. It will go away after a while."

I wasn't too sure about myself but I knew better than to mention it. Double vision or no, Gibby would have taken the wheel. I know the boy. If forced to it, he would even attempt to drive two cars along two roads. I didn't want any part of that. Happily the doctors were on my side and they had the State cops with them. They set us down as a menace to highway safety and assigned a man to do our driving for us till we were back across the state line. As a courtesy, they offered us his services the rest of the way as well but, so far as Connecticut roads were concerned, they gave us no choice.

It was a happy arrangement. Once we were in the

car and on the road, shock and brandy added up together for the inevitable effect. Both Gibby and I corked off and we slept all the way back to town. We were already down into Manhattan when I woke, and since Gibby showed no sign of waking, it fell to me to tell our chauffeur where we wanted to go. I directed him to Gibby's place. I even enlisted his assistance for a project of carrying Gibby out of the car and up to his apartment and his bed.

I thought I had the rest of the night all taped out. Not that there was too much of it left, as nights go, but then I had just come awake and I wasn't up to too much planning either. The way it went was that we would get Gibby up to his place and put him to bed. Then I would call a doctor who was a pal of ours, just for a New York opinion on Gibby's head. I planned only one more call. That one would be to the Homicide boys down at Police Headquarters. I was going to tell them what I knew and let them take it from there till morning.

It was a sensible program and the part I'd thought would be trickiest went sensibly enough. I remembered to fish the keys to Gibby's apartment out of his pocket before we lifted him out of the car. He didn't stir or even mumble while we were carrying him and I didn't know whether to be thankful that it was going so well or to worry about the possibility that he had dropped into some form of unconsciousness more drastic than sleep. With every step we carried the totally inert, dead weight of that big lug, I was attaching greater and greater importance to having that New York medical opinion on the damage to his head.

With the gentlest care we lowered him to the bed.

197

The Connecticut cop started on his shirt buttons while I tackled shoelaces. The laces were still wet and that made the knots hard to handle. I hadn't made any headway with handling them when Gibby kicked me lightly in the chin, slapped the cop's hand away from the first shirt button, sat up in bed, and reached for the phone.

"Thanks for carrying me," he said. "I enjoyed every moment of it, but enough's enough. The gay round of pleasure stops right here. We have to get back to work."

"If you want to do your own phoning," I said, "it's all right with me. Call Sam. Tell him we want him over here on the double."

Sam, of course, was that medic whose opinion I wanted.

Gibby grinned at me. "You don't need Sam," he said. "You've never been better in your life. Your hand is as steady as a pickpocket's and your strength is as the strength of ten. You didn't drop me even once."

He had been playing possum all the time. I ignored it.

"I want Sam to look at your head," I insisted.

"He's seen it lots of times."

Gibby spun the dial. He wasn't calling Sam. He called Homicide and got himself put through to Harrity. There was an extension out in the living room and I went out and picked it up. It wasn't that I had any ideas of letting Gibby carry the ball again that night, not if I could prevent it. I took the phone with exactly that purpose of prevention in mind. I wanted to hear anything Harrity had for us because I was dead set on finding all the arguments I could for letting further action go till morning.

It started out well enough.

"I have news for you," he said. "You and Connecticut both asking for a bright red sedan with much much chromium, brightest star in the Jellicoe fleet. We've got that baby."

"Complete with driver?" Gibby asked eagerly.

I started rehearsing the routine I would give him about letting the man stew in a cell till morning. Harrity answered and I quit rehearsing.

"No driver," he said. "Just the car. It's nicely parked and all locked up. It's on Jerome Avenue up in the Bronx, right by the end of the subway line. We have it staked out. If anybody comes to drive it away, we'll have him, and you and Connecticut can toss him up for grabs."

Gibby sighed. "Nobody will be coming to drive it away," he said. "It's a waste of manpower staking it out."

"Connecticut's request," Harrity said.

"It's not their manpower," Gibby muttered. "They can afford to waste it. What else? What about that New York car I asked for?"

"Registration you phoned in from up there?" Harrity said. "We've got that. Car belongs to a dame. Mabel Sylvester, lives in the East Fifties." He reeled off the address.

Have you ever been on the phone and had the bird at the other end suddenly decide he's through talking and that he can let you know as much by slamming the telephone down in the cradle. It's a sound that makes your eardrum jump. Mine jumped and I was rubbing my ear when Gibby came charging out of the bedroom with that Connecticut cop who had driven us down from Westport thundering at his heels. I caught at Gibby as he whizzed past.

"Where are you going?" I shouted. "You're off your head."

The best I could do was hang on to him and let him carry me along. There wasn't any stopping him. We did have a pause out at the elevator. It took a moment or two for the car to come up even though Gibby never took his thumb off the bell button.

"Four murders is enough," he growled. "With luck we might still make it to stop a fifth, but even now it will only be with luck."

"Couldn't Harrity go?"

"There isn't that much luck, not nearly enough to cover all the time it would take to fill Harrity in."

We piled into the car and Gibby gave the directions. That kid from Westport was one terrific driver. He never took a corner on more than two wheels and he zipped through the straightaway bits so fast that we never did settle back to all four. He handled that car as though it were a five-passenger motorcycle. When Gibby told him to pull up it was in front of one of a row of white-painted brick houses. Dawn was something between pink and yellow at the end of the street and the whole row of houses—blank and decently asleep, of course, at that hour—looked as though they were made of old ivory touched with water color. These were fine old houses and it was a good street.

Gibby catapulted out of the car and ran up the steps to lean on the doorbell with that same insistence he had used on the elevator call button back at his own place. Nothing happened. He kept his finger on the bell, but he began eying the neat, black-painted wood of the door.

"I think we can make it by that window on the left," he said. "If we can't we'll break down the door."

The window on the left looked all too easy. This house was one of those old-fashioned English basement jobs that you used to find all over town. Most of them were brownstones but the older ones were brick and the brick jobs have been back in fashion for several years. Breaking down doors and going in windows doesn't rate as standard operating procedure for our office under any conditions. In this sort of street and this sort of house it is always the better part of wisdom to tread lightly and cautiously. People who live in these houses are people who retain the kind of legal talent that can make an Assistant DA wish he'd never been born. I've seen them do it on lesser provocation than a job of illegal entry.

"Give people time to wake up and climb out of bed and come downstairs," I said.

"A woman can be strangled quicker than that," Gibby growled and came away from the bell.

He was measuring the distance to the window.

"You're not going in that window," I said.

"I can make it easily," Gibby answered. "You just have to give me a leg up."

"I'm not giving you any leg up."

He turned away from me in disgust. "Just a quick boost," he said to our Westport lad.

The boy was a cop and he wasn't a complete fool. He looked from Gibby to me and back to Gibby again.

"Please, sir," he said. "It's not like you had a warrant or like that, sir. And me. I'm not even in my own territory. I don't know if I even ought to be here at all. My orders was to drive you to the state line or home if you wanted, that's all."

Gibby didn't take the time for further argument. He charged up the steps and back to the front door. With a running lunge he drove his shoulder against the wood. It was a good door. It didn't even rattle. He pulled back for another drive at it. I looked at his face. Even in that early light that was putting a pink glow on everything, his face looked ghastly. It was that grainy sort of white you'll see in the ash of a good cigar. On a cigar it looks good. On Gibby it looked frightening.

I know when I'm licked. I took his arm and pulled him down the steps.

"We'll go in the window," I said.

Gibby forced a smile. "Just a leg up and I'll come around and open the door," he said.

I wasn't that licked. I went to work on Westport. I didn't try to kid him that this was legal or anything like that. I just told him nobody would ever know he had even been with us. All he had to do was give first me and then Gibby a boost up to the window and then he was to take off and forget he had ever been with us beyond driving us home. Between us, Gibby and I chivvied the poor boy into position by the iron gate that served as the basement entrance. That put him directly under the window.

I thought I should have trouble with Gibby at that point about who was going in first, but I might have known better. Gibby has a perfect sense of just how far he can push me. He stood by while the cop boosted me up. I caught the window ledge and pulled myself over it. One glance told me I was in an empty room. I began feeling better. I told myself it would be an empty house.

Well-heeled householders not yet returned from their summer holidaying. The house was that quiet. I turned back to the window in time to help Gibby over the sill.

We stood together in that quiet house and caught our breaths. The morning light was still too thin to see the room anything but most dimly. You didn't have to see it at all clearly, however, to know that it was all delicacy and elegance. I had the impression of silk and of perfume and of things that were soft and finely wrought. There was only one door to the room and that was closed.

Gibby moved toward it. He wasn't making a sound. I crept along with him. We reached the door and opened it. It brought us to the entrance hall—cool, austere, all black and white. The floor was tiled in big squares that alternated the black with the white, but just inside the entrance door lay something that was all black. Gibby reached out and touched a light switch. A soft glow materialized from somewhere. It was one of those extra fancy jobs of concealed and diffused lighting. If you are setting a thing like this up for yourself, you may prefer a sharper light, but the glow was enough for then.

The something that was all black was a woman. She was wearing a black suit that looked like one of those treasures Sydney Bell's cleaning woman had described so knowingly, and the contrast of the color of her skin to the black of her suit was at least as dramatic as was the contrast in the black and white tiling on which she lay. Even though the light was hardly adequate for police work, it was enough to show her face and that was white with the special whiteness of death, and on her bare throat stood the blue and purplish bruises, the marks of manual strangulation.

Running to her side, we clattered across the tile. Gibby bent to touch her.

"I was hoping against hope," he said, "but I should have known we would be much too late. We never had a chance of getting here in time."

"Gone cold?" I asked.

"Dead a good hour," Gibby answered.

I had so many questions that I was trying to fasten on which I should ask first. Who was this woman? How had Gibby known she was slated to be the next strangling? Where in the crowded happenings of that day and night had he found a timetable for all this?

I might have started on one of the questions or another. I don't know, because at just that moment the silent house was shaken with a resounding, metallic clash.

Gibby dodged around the woman's body and wrenched the front door open. I'm ashamed to say I haven't any idea of how I reached the door. I may have gone around the body or I may have vaulted across it. I don't even know that just then I was even remembering that it lay there. Gibby and I erupted into the street.

In the little basement area where the Westport cop had stood to give us a leg up to the window he was still standing, but now he stood embattled. It was a resoundingly noisy battle because the heavy, wrought-iron basement gate now stood ajar and the struggle kept throwing the combatants against it to slam it again and again.

Locked in combat with Westport was Milton Bannerman, and that was pretty even. Outside forces, however, were tipping the odds in Bannerman's favor, but only slightly. These outside forces were Joan Loomis' fists. She was pounding the officer's head and shoulders with them and her right fist was wrapped in a white handkerchief. Just before we dove in to break it up, Bannerman shifted his hands for a better hold on Westport and I noticed that around his right he had wrapped the torn rags of a white handkerchief.

eight

Up to this point, of course, our ally from across the state line had had every reason for wanting to bow out and as quickly as possible. By the time we had disengaged the poor fellow from his entanglement with the River Forks love birds, however, every last one of his worst fears had been realized and he had nothing more to lose.

As Westport saw it, we were dangerous company. He had come through thus far unscathed—his wrestling with Bannerman hadn't gone beyond rumpling his uniform and the blows Joan Loomis had rained upon him had bounced off harmlessly enough—but he was laying it all to luck and he had no wish to strain his luck further. He left us. We went back into the house, taking our captives with us. They were a rather soiled and rumpled pair, but that was nothing to the way Gibby and I looked. We were still half-wet from our sojourn in the brook up at Westport.

I put through the usual calls—police, Medical Examiner, the routine. I was beginning to lose count of how many times I had done this in something less than twenty-four hours but I had a feeling that the boys on the headquarters switchboard were getting to the place where they would be needing no more than the sound of my voice in their headsets to set them automatically to sending out the meat wagon.

Even in the couple of moments I was on the phone Gibby made a start on our precious pair of holier-than-thous.

"You have an awful lot to tell us," he said.

"I don't even know where to begin," said Joan Loomis.

"We don't have much," said Milton Bannerman. "We have a lot less than you think."

Gibby fixed him with a cold look. "Anything less than I'm thinking," he said, "isn't going to be enough. You need plenty. You need enough to get the two of you out from under five murders and two attempted murders. This is a massacre. Talk and talk fast."

"Five murders?" Bannerman bleated. "Ellie and Miss Sylvester."

"And Harry and George and a nice cop up in Connecticut," Gibby said. "Start with Miss Sylvester."

Bannerman's lips set in a thin line. "She was a horrible woman," he said savagely. "She got not half of what she deserved."

The girl cried out. "Milton," she protested. "Don't. The woman's dead."

"I know she's dead," Milton stormed. "And she died just the same way Ellie died. I know that and I know there isn't any justice in it. Think of what Ellie was and think of what she was. Ellie got no more than she deserved and, compared with this woman, even Ellie was the spotless lamb."

"Milton," the girl whimpered. "Please, Milton."

"The wages of sin," Gibby said.

Bannerman rounded on him. Gibby might have been the accused and Bannerman the accuser.

"Don't sneer at it," he snarled. "It's the truth. Don't sneer at the truth."

"I'm not sneering at it," Gibby said. "I'm waiting for it. When I told you to talk, I wasn't asking for a lecture on your moral principles. I want to know how you got here. I want to know why you came. I want to know what happened, everything that happened."

"I followed Joan. That woman brought her here."

It was an answer, but it lacked detail. Gibby gave him an illustration of what might be a more adequate answer.

"Joan left the hotel shortly after we sent the two of you back there," Gibby said. "You followed her. You followed her to Grand Central Station where she picked up a man named George. Joan and George left the station together and you were still following them. Take it from there. I want all of it, step by step."

"I followed Joan and this man. I didn't know his name. They went to a house in a part of town I'd never seen before."

"Could you find your way back to the house or was it this house?"

"It wasn't this house. It was on the other side of town from here. They only went as far as the outside of the place and they didn't go in. The place was full of police. Police cars out front, officers all over. The man saw that and he pulled Joan away. He took her back to the corner and took her into a saloon."

"I had plain ginger ale," Joan put in defensively.

"I know you didn't drink anything but you shouldn't have been in that place at all. You shouldn't have been with that man."

"I shouldn't have ever come to New York," Joan said.

"I was crazy to let you come. How I could have been such a fool! I'll never know how I could have let her deceive me all these years."

"Milton, please." The girl was pleading with him.

"That's right," Gibby put in. " 'Milton, please.' We haven't the time for should and shouldn't. She went into the bar with this man George. Then what? Did you go in after them?"

"No. There was a big glass front and I could watch them from outside. The man left her alone at the table for a minute or two and then he came back and they talked. He tried to take her hand a couple of times, but Joan wouldn't let him."

"That's because she was drinking only ginger ale," Gibby muttered. "Then what happened?"

"Then Miss Sylvester came."

"She was driving a car?"

"No. No car."

"How did she come then? Taxi?"

"No. She was walking. I would never have noticed her if she had come in a car or a taxi. I wasn't standing there watching just any woman that came by. I don't do that and anyhow I was watching Joan. It was Joan I was worrying about."

"Naturally, but you did notice Miss Sylvester. Why was that? Was it because she was like Joan? Was it . . ."

Bannerman lowered his head and charged at Gibby.

"Don't say that," he bellowed. "Don't you dare say that."

I grabbed him and shoved him back in his chair. The bell rang and Gibby went to let the boys in and to brief them on our latest murder while I worked at telling Bannerman to behave himself.

Gibby returned and finished his question. "Did you notice Miss Sylvester," he asked, "because she was also someone you knew, someone you had to worry about?"

"She was nobody. She was nothing to me. I had never seen her before in my life."

"But you did notice her. Why?"

"I noticed her because she came popping out of this alley that was right alongside the saloon. She startled me. One minute there was nobody around and the next she came popping out of the alley. You don't expect women to come popping at you out of alleys, leastways you don't expect it of women like her, all silk and perfume and that stuff."

"She startled you?"

"She did. She popped out of the alley and she came

past me and went into the saloon. Inside she stood for a moment looking for someone and then she went right over to the table where Joan and this man were sitting. She sat down. The man left the table and went to the back of the place. He never came back. I didn't see him again. Joan and Miss Sylvester came out and I ducked around the corner into the alley and watched them. Miss Sylvester was trying to get a taxi. I ran to the corner and got one. I waited till I saw them in a taxi and then I told my man to follow them. I followed them here."

"Then what?"

"They came here and they went inside. I waited in the street a while and I couldn't stand it. I went up and rang the bell. She let me in, Miss Sylvester, I mean. That's all."

"Not by a long shot," Gibby said.

"How I got here. Why I came."

"And everything that happened. Miss Sylvester was presumably alive when she let you in. When we came along and rang the bell, nobody let us in. Not Miss Sylvester, not Miss Loomis, not you. Miss Sylvester was dead by then and that lets her out of explaining her actions. Nothing lets Miss Loomis out and nothing lets you out."

"All right," Bannerman said sulkily. "Not that we know anything except the kind of woman she was. We were here upstairs, talking to her. The bell rang. She left us and went down to answer the bell. She didn't come back. We waited and waited and after a while we went down to look for her. She was down in the hall where you found her. She'd been killed like Ellie. Then you rang the bell. We didn't want any part of this. It wasn't any of our business except maybe the way it hooked up with Ellie and not even that way now because now I know and I'm not having any part of Ellie either. Alive or dead, she's not my sister any more. She hasn't been all these last years. I've washed my hands of her."

"Which makes them clean enough to suit you perhaps," Gibby told him. "They're going to have to be clean enough to suit the law before any of this can stop being your business, Milton."

"I have nothing to hide and nothing to fear," Bannerman said, striking an attitude.

"That's a help," Gibby said. "Since you have nothing to hide, stop hiding it. A man who had nothing to hide would have opened the door to us."

Joan took a hand. "We had no way of knowing it was you," she said. "It could have been this—this killer —coming back."

"So you tiptoed downstairs and waited till you heard us in the house up here. Then you tried to sneak away by the basement entrance."

"All right," Bannerman said defiantly. "So we did. Is that so terrible? We were through with all of this. We're leaving this town and we're never coming back. Waiting till I can take Ellie home and bury her—that's out. I wouldn't put her beside decent people and make no mistake about that. Our parents, they were decent people. I knew what it would mean if we got involved with you on this woman's death. It would mean questions and delays and more questions and delays. We'd been through all that. We'd had enough."

"And you were washing your hands of all of it," Gibby said. "We knew Miss Loomis' passion for cleanliness, but now you've got it, too. You were quite a while upstairs after you found the body. You took all the time you needed to wipe everything you might have touched in this house. There were going to be no fingerprints for us to find, neither yours nor Miss Loomis'."

"That isn't so," Bannerman growled.

"Milton, please," Joan Loomis protested.

" 'Milton, please,' " Gibby said, echoing her again. "You both had your handkerchiefs wrapped around your hands. That was so you wouldn't be leaving any fingerprints on the gate downstairs when you went out. You can be contemptuous as you like about the local moral standards. Don't be too contemptuous of our intelligence."

"So we didn't want to be involved," Bannerman said. "Show me one decent man or woman who wouldn't recoil from the very thought of being involved with people like that."

"You're slipping back into moral judgments," Gibby said. "We're still on facts."

"You have all the facts."

"You were here a long time talking with Miss Sylvester. What were you talking about?"

"Ellie, and that's a closed book."

"We haven't closed it. We don't close them till the killer has been tried and convicted and executed."

"That's your affair. I'm not interested."

"Then you're going to be bored. You have no choice. This woman told you that your sister wasn't what she'd pretended to be. If she was a model at all, she had used her modeling only as a cover for her real profession of call girl."

216

"She told me that my sister was a whore," Bannerman said.

He preferred not to discuss this at all, but if he was to speak of it, he wouldn't shelter behind any euphemisms. If the word was in Scriptures, it was good enough for Milton Bannerman.

"This was the first you knew it?"

Bannerman turned on Gibby a look of withering contempt. "Of course it was the first I knew it," he said. "You saw how I was mourning her. When you took me down to see her body, if I had known it then, I wouldn't have cried for her. I would have spit on her."

"Milton," Joan Loomis gasped.

"That's the truth. He wanted the truth. All right, he has it."

"And," Gibby added, "if you had known it earlier, you would have killed her yourself. You would have killed her with your own two hands."

"I would," Bannerman said. "I would have killed her for what she had become, for lying to me the way she did, for daring to bring Joan into that harlot's den of hers. I would have enjoyed killing her."

Joan rose out of her chair, walked across to her fiancé and planted on his cheek a slap that was the resoundingly lusty mate to the one she had given him in Grand Central Station.

"That's quite enough of that," she said firmly. "I'm not excusing Ellie. I'm not excusing anyone, but I'm not excusing myself either. Most of this is my fault. I've been the world's worst fool, but I've learned better. I've seen what a fool I've been, and I'm quite over that. There will be no more foolishness."

217

"We observed that you learn fast," Gibby told her. "After Ellie's killing you quite forgot about removing your fingerprints. You remembered everything else but you forgot that, but you don't make the same mistake twice. Here, after Miss Sylvester's killing, you were careful about fingerprints."

The girl blushed, but she stood her ground. "I deserved that," she said. "But that was the least of what I've learned, Mr. Gibson. I don't think you can begin to conceive of what a fool I was, how much I had to learn."

Gibby laughed. "We already know that your education did progress to the point where you knew how to pick up a man in a railroad station and go to a bar with him even if you drank nothing but ginger ale," he said. "We have a pretty good idea of how much you learned."

The girl didn't flinch. What she might have had to say to that crack, we'll never know, because Bannerman started another one of his charges at Gibby and she moved to hold Bannerman down and then just at that point we had an interruption. A man had come up to the house and rung the bell. The cops had let this early caller in and asked him his business. Now they brought him in to us.

It was the big boy, K. R. E. Jellicoe, and I had never seen him looking so well. It might have been that blue suited him better than had the browns he had been wearing the previous afternoon and it might also have been that the morning light did more for him than had those glaring arcs under which the Bellevue surgeon had been working at slapping on the adhesive tape. In any event, he was wearing a neat, blue suit and blue shirt and blue tie and impeccable black shoes. He looked rosy and suntanned, not the yellow that had first drawn my eye to him. He did still have a surgical dressing on his face but it was a neat, white patch, neatly fastened down.

He recognized us, and a couple of familiar faces after the cops out in the hall apparently hit him as a welcome sight. We might have been a pair of his long-lost brothers. He went right into his story.

"Gosh," he said. "You two. At least you'll know what I'm talking about. I'm trying to find my car. Remember yesterday? You were there. It was outside that store. I met these two fellows I knew and they pulled a fastie on me. It wasn't the first time. They're always doing it. You see, I'd had a couple of drinks and they're right enough because sometimes when I have drinks in me I don't drive so good. What they do is they'll get my car away from me and they put it away. Then, when I'm all sobered up and it's safe for me to drive it again, they tell me where they've put it. It was like that yesterday afternoon and it was just as well because I did tie one on last night but now it's morning and I'm sober as a judge and I'd like my car. I went around to one of them, his apartment, last night, fellow named George. I slept there and he didn't come in all night so I figured this morning I'd go around to Harry's and get my car from him. He's the other fellow."

"I know," Gibby said. "You've been around to Harry's?"

"I've just been there. He isn't there. There's nobody there but the super and he told me Harry was killed last night. So naturally I came right over here to tell Mae and now they say she's been killed, too. Are they kidding me or what?"

"They're not kidding you, Mr. Jellicoe," Gibby said.

"Gee. I'm sorry about Harry and I'm sorry about

Mae. We had a lot of laughs together them and me, but what about my car? If George doesn't turn up, how do I find my car?"

"George isn't going to turn up."

"George? What's happened to George?"

"George got it, too. He was killed last night, like Harry, like Mae, like Sydney Bell."

"Yeah, I heard about her, poor kid. But Harry and Mae and now George, too. Has somebody gone crazy or what?"

"Crazy or what," Gibby said. "It's been a massacre. Mac, here, and myself, we were near misses." He turned and indicated Bannerman and the girl. "You know these people?" he asked.

Jellicoe shook his head. "No," he said. "Can't say I do. The young lady I did see once. She was on Broadway with Sydney but we didn't meet."

Gibby did introductions.

"Kirk Jellicoe," he said. "Milton Bannerman, Sydney's brother."

Jellicoe missed on the Bannerman completely.

He stuck out his hand. "I'm sorry, Mr. Bell," he said. "I'm sorry about your sister. She was a good kid."

Bannerman looked stonily at the hand and made no move to take it. "She was a . . ." he began. Joan Loomis caught him with a warning look and he never finished the sentence. It made no difference to Gibby or to me. We knew the word he hadn't spoken. Jellicoe looked bewildered and, as he put his hand away, he looked a little bit hurt. He was almost pouting.

"Mr. Bannerman," Gibby explained, "didn't approve of the way his sister earned her living. He doesn't want

220

any part of her memory or of any of her associates. You were one of her associates, weren't you?"

Jellicoe smiled. "She was a good kid," he said. "We had some good parties."

Bannerman was charging again. This time he was headed for Jellicoe. Joan made a try at stopping him but he knocked her aside, and Gibby and I had to catch him and hold him down. Joan fell and Jellicoe, who was quicker than you'd think for a man of his bulk, jumped forward and caught her. He helped her to her feet. She thanked him primly and stepped away from him. His hands fluttered after her with teasing affection but she sidestepped them. He dropped his hands and stood back and smiled at her. I shouted and a couple of the officers came in from the hall.

Gibby let me give the orders, and I told them to ride herd on our wild man. They shoved Bannerman down into a chair and stood either side of him. Gibby nodded approval.

Jellicoe touched Gibby's elbow. "Now about my car," he said.

"Stick around," Gibby told him. "We'll turn it up for you. We've already found the other one, the red sedan."

"The sedan? That's up home in the garage."

"It was. It's in the Bronx now."

"But I locked the garage. I know I locked it. I always lock it. You mean someone broke in?"

"The door's open," Gibby said. "The lock's broken. The sedan's parked in the Bronx and one hell of a nice Westport cop is dead."

Jellicoe blinked. He counted on his fingers. "Sydney," he said, adding them up, "Mae, Harry, George, and you say a cop up home. I guess I shouldn't be bothering you with my troubles. After all, it's only cars and they make new ones all the time. Good kids, now, they don't make those all the time, not like Sydney was, they don't. I'll buzz off and bother someone else with my troubles. You've got your hands full."

Gibby gave him the big smile. "We have our hands full," he said. "You're right about that. We don't want them any fuller though. We've had five killings and we're stopping with that. We're not going to have a sixth. I'm speaking plainly, Mr. Jellicoe. Sydney Bell was what her brother has called a whore."

Jellicoe turned a reproachful look on Bannerman. "That's no kind of name to be calling a good kid like her," he said. "She had fun and she gave a man a good time. What's so wrong with that?"

Bannerman turned purple and his pair of cops moved in a bit closer. He looked down at the floor and said nothing.

"Mr. Bannerman thinks it's wrong," Gibby said. "So wrong that he thinks that he, being her brother, had every right to kill her with his own two hands. Do I have to draw you a picture? She was strangled. Harry and George have been strangled and, since Mr. Bannerman started the plain speaking, we can go on with it. They were a pair of pimps. Let's face it, Mr. Jellicoe. The girl is gone. Her pimps are gone. Mae is gone and Mae was running a call girl deal with Sydney Bell at the top of the list. So who is left? You're left, Mr. Jellicoe, the man in Sydney Bell's life. How does that make your neck feel? The cop up in Westport is dead

222

for nothing at all, only because he got in the way. If you die, Mr. Jellicoe, it won't be for nothing. It will be for laughs, for those laughs you and Sydney Bell had together."

Jellicoe sat down. He was staring at Bannerman. Bannerman glared back at him and I began wondering whether two cops were enough.

"He is crazy," Jellicoe said.

Joan Loomis darted forward. She stood in front of the big man and stamped her foot.

"He isn't," she screamed. "He has every right to be, but he isn't. He hasn't done anything. He hasn't killed anybody. He didn't even know these people. He never suspected."

She turned to Gibby and she talked. She needed no prompting or prodding. She had her story to tell and it poured out of her.

She had come to New York in her full prayer-meeting-and-church-supper River Forks innocence. New York had been a shock and Ellie Bannerman had been a worse shock. It wasn't that she had known then what Ellie Bannerman was. She would never have set foot in Ellie's apartment if she had known that or, having gone there and finding out, she would not have remained there another moment. That she hadn't known, but she had seen right away that Ellie was not the girl she had made herself seem in her letters to her brother or in her visits to River Forks.

Ellie had been fast. That had been evident. There were all the ways Joan could tell. The liquor in the apartment and Ellie drinking it. Cigarettes and Ellie smoking them. Her clothes—the filmy red nightgowns

and the black lace underthings, the way she talked to
people on the telephone, calling everyone darling even
when it was men who called.

Joan had been distressed. She hadn't even begun to
suspect the actual truth, but she had been unhappy that
a nice girl like Ellie should behave in this way that
made her seem anything but a nice girl. She had been
unhappy and she had worried. She had been glad to
get away to Boston, but she had taken her worries with
her. Milt was coming to New York. Milt would see
what his sister was like. Ellie had made that clear to
Joan. She was a big girl now and Milt was a big boy.
He was getting married and he would be living his own
life. She was living hers and she was tired of putting
on an act for Milt. It was time he learned what the
world was like and learned to accept it. This was the
way people lived away from River Forks and Ellie was
through with River Forks forever.

All this was going to be a terrible shock to Milt, and
Joan, even when she had thought it had been nothing
but smoking and drinking and clothes, had worried
about how he was going to take it. Then Joan came back
from Boston on that late train. She came up to the apartment. Ellie had given her a key and she let herself in.

She got that far with it and she faltered. She had
gone very pale and she looked as though she were
about to be sick. Gibby took her arm and gently led
her to a chair.

"Take it easy," he said. "It's almost as rough in the
telling as it was in the doing. Take it easy."

She looked up at him. "You know what I did?" she
murmured.

"I had a good hunch of it when we first met last night," Gibby told her. "Once we'd fingerprinted you, I knew it was better than a hunch. It was a sure thing."

He let her rest a bit while he told her what she had done. She had come into the apartment and had found there all the evidences of what had been a bacchanalia. She had found liquor glasses and liquor bottles and tumbled bedclothes and amid the tumbled bedclothes she had found Ellie Bannerman, dead and cold in her bed. She had seen the purple marks of strangulation on Ellie's throat. She had seen the sheer red nightgown Ellie was wearing and the way the nightgown was and she had known everything then. She had known that Ellie had been what her brother was now calling her.

Her heart had broken for the dead girl, but she had known that it would be breaking again.

"Actually you were hoping that it could break again," Gibby told her. "You were hoping that when Milt would come and see this, it would all be new to him even though you knew that it would be so bad that he couldn't take it. You were hoping that it was like that, but you were terribly afraid it wasn't. You were terribly afraid that he had come, that he had arrived ahead of time, had found his sister and had forced her to tell him that she was just what she was. You were terribly afraid that Milton had killed her."

"I was a fool," the girl moaned. "I should have known better."

"How should you have known? He said so himself. He would kill her with his own two hands."

Gibby went on with it, and as he reconstructed for her step by step just what she had done, the girl denied nothing and corrected nothing. He had the whole sequence and he had it in complete, circumstantial detail. Telling herself that she could steel herself to make the whole thing look very different, make it look so different that Milt Bannerman need never know the bitter truth about his sister, she had braced herself for what she thought she had to do. She had fought down the thought that Milt Bannerman might already know, that Milt might have killed his sister, for either way there would be this thing she was making herself do, whether to protect him from knowledge or to protect him from the consequences of his act.

"The wages of sin are death," Gibby said. "You had heard that too often and you couldn't get it out of your head. You knew so exactly what would be. The police would come. They would find the dead girl. She had sinned and she had been killed for it because the wages of sin are death. We would look for the most likely person to have paid Ellie Bannerman those wages and where could we look but to her brother?"

"I didn't really believe it even then," the girl said, sobbing. "No matter how it looked, I didn't really believe it and now I know. He didn't come ahead of time, not that much ahead of time. He never knew at all. I tried to protect him from ever knowing. Was I so wrong?"

"Don't ask me," Gibby said. "Ask Milt. He's the moral standards man. He'll tell you the truth must prevail."

He returned to his reconstruction. Joan Loomis had locked the door. The television had been on low and she had left it on because it would screen the noise of what she was to do in the apartment. Then she had cleaned the place up. She had cleaned it thoroughly.

She had made a parcel of liquor bottles and glasses and bar fixings and ash trays and cigarettes and lighters and matches. She had made a clean sweep of all these minor appurtenances of sin. Then she had gone through the closets and the drawers. She had removed all the sinful garments, all the black lace, all the pink satin, all the strapless, backless, frontless, sleeveless, clinging jobs. She had made a clean sweep, leaving only suits and the coat which, however fashionable, would still seem decent in the austere eye of Milton Bannerman.

Then had come the worst thing she had to do. She had to get Ellie out of that sinful, sheer red nightgown. She had made herself do it. She had taken the nylon and lace off the body and had put the body into a night-dress out of her own luggage, the cute and demure job that had been on the body when the cleaning woman had found it. She had buttoned the thing all the way up to the throat. That made Ellie look so much better. It covered the horror of the welts on her throat and it also avoided the indecency of even one undone button. She had made the bed up fresh and had arranged the body primly in it.

The closets and the drawers looked unnaturally empty and she had helped that with the prayer book and the tracts and a few of her own prim things that she had been buying for her trousseau. Somewhere in the course of all this, she had been sick. She had leaned over the washstand in the bathroom and had hung on for dear life while her stomach gave back everything that had been in it. She had cleaned up after herself but she had not been too knowing in her clean-up. It had never occurred to her to remove fingerprints.

When she had left the apartment, she had turned

off the television and had taken with her her parcel of the liquor and tobacco things and, crammed into her own luggage, she had carried off all the seductive lovelies that had been in Ellie's wardrobe. The job had been done and, so far as she knew, she hadn't been seen or heard.

"But you weren't quite finished," Gibby told her. "You were in a spot. The easiest thing would have been to dump everything of hers down the incinerator as you had dumped the liquor and the glasses and the cigarettes and the ash trays and all that. You would have liked to dump the clothes as well but you couldn't. You had to have a hotel room. You had to have money to carry you along till Milton would come. You had put your nightdress on the body and your underwear in the drawer. You had bought the nightdress and those underclothes up in Boston and your cousin up there knew you had shopped them. You had to have something to show for that shopping and you had no money. You could have taken the money out of Ellie's purse. She had more than enough there for your day's needs, but you couldn't make yourself do that. It would have been stealing. Taking the clothes wasn't stealing. That was protecting Milton. Since they had to be gotten rid of somehow and you had to get a bit of money somehow without stealing it . . ."

At that point the girl did interrupt him, but not to deny any of these acts he was charging her with.

"I did see the money in her purse," she said. "I saw it when I was taking her cigarettes and matches out to dispose of them with the ash trays and liquor and all that stuff, but I wasn't thinking about money then. I was only thinking about what I had to do in the apart-

228

ment. When I had everything done and I had crowded her clothes into my suitcases along with my own, I had the other things—the liquor and the cigarettes—in a paper bag. I turned off the television and the lights and I went out to the hall and dumped the paper bag down the incinerator. I wanted to put her clothes down there, too, but I couldn't. If anyone had come along, it would have looked too strange. The other things could just have been a bag of rubbish, but to open my cases and take out the clothes and feed them into the incinerator would have been different. I knew I had to get rid of them but I thought I could dump them somewhere. I went down to the street and looked for a cab. When I checked in my purse for the cab fare, it came to me that I had to have money now for a hotel and to get me through the day and to buy things to replace what I had left in Ellie's place, the things I'd bought in Boston and that my cousin up there had seen. I had seen the same things in New York but more expensive. I knew just where to go to find them, but I didn't have nearly enough money for all that and I couldn't make myself go back up there to take Ellie's money."

"That was when you saw the secondhand-clothes shop," Gibby said, "and that saved you from having to go back to the apartment. As soon as it opened in the morning, you went around there and sold all of Ellie's clothes. You sold them cheap and the woman in the shop thought she was getting a terrific bargain and she was asking no questions. It wasn't the first time she had bought stolen goods and she knew how to behave. Even though she gave you only a fraction of even secondhand value, it was enough. You were able to go to the hotel. You were able to eat yesterday and to shop all day and pick up replacements for the things you had left as camouflage at Ellie's." He stopped and waited for her to speak. She said nothing. "Do you want to correct any of that?" he asked. "Have I got it wrong at any point?"

"It's as though you'd been there all the time watching me," the girl said. "I was an idiot."

"You were an idiot," Gibby agreed. "You would have been the world's worst idiot to do all that, put yourself through that ordeal, run those fantastic risks for nothing more than to save poor, pure Milton from ever knowing about his sister's life. You can't expect us to believe that you were that much of an idiot. You made yourself do it to protect him from the consequences of murder, because it was murder and you didn't have the first doubt that he had done it."

"I was an idiot. I know better now. It wasn't Milt."

I looked at Milton Bannerman crouched in his chair between the two watchful cops and I pitied this girl. It was as though Bannerman hadn't even heard a word of the ordeal she had been through. It was as though it hadn't mattered a bit to him that she had endured everything and risked everything in her effort to save him. He wasn't sparing her so much as a glance. His eyes never moved. They were fixed on K. R. E. Jellicoe and I have never seen a hotter blaze of hate in any man's eyes.

Gibby was talking again. He was still reconstructing, telling Joan Loomis the full story that she hadn't had the strength to tell him. As she had gone through her day, she had become aware of the fact that most of the day a man or a couple of men had been following her. She had noticed them and she had been annoyed by them, but she hadn't thought that it was anything more than

New York's sinful ways, nothing more than the sort of thing that had brought Ellie Bannerman from her pure beginnings to her dreadful death. In the course of the afternoon she had gone back to the neighborhood of Ellie's apartment. She hadn't gone in but she had seen the police about and she knew then that the body had been found. Somewhere about that time she had lost the men who had been following her.

Joan looked up at Gibby. "What I did in the apartment," she said. "I can understand that. I did leave my fingerprints on everything. You would know how to see through every move I made. But this? How could you know about the men and how could you know just where I lost them and when?"

I was glad she asked the question. I didn't have to save it to ask Gibby later.

His answer couldn't have been simpler. That part of it had been luck. The men who had been following her had been procurers and blackmailers. They had been to Sydney Bell's apartment before Joan had gone there. They had known that Sydney was dead. Sydney alive had been a source of profit to them. They had not been men who would give up easily on a chance of profit. They had hoped that Sydney dead might continue to be a source of profit. They had been watching the apartment. They had seen Joan come to it. They had known how long she had been there. They had seen her go. They had followed her. They had seen her sell the clothes. We knew how easily one could see through the window into that shop.

"They were keeping an eye on you," Gibby said. "Mr. Jellicoe says he saw you once on Broadway with this woman you knew as Ellie Bannerman, the girl they called Sydney Bell. It is a cinch that they'd seen you with her some time or another. They would know who you were. They would be waiting for you to lead them to Sydney Bell's brother. They were looking for profit."

"But I did lose them for a while, for the rest of the afternoon and until I went to the station. Why did they leave me then? How did they know where and when to pick me up again?"

"Your boy friend's wages of sin seem to have put me in the mood for proverbs," Gibby said. " 'A bird in the hand.' You know that one. That was a matter of accident. They were following you and you took them past the shop where you had sold Ellie's things. Mr. Jellicoe happened to be in the shop just then. He had taken a few drinks and was in a sentimental mood. He had spotted a very special red nylon and lace nightgown in the window and it was a nightgown he knew too well. He went in and bought it as a souvenir. Your men saw him do it and they left you. They knew your hotel. They knew when Milton's train was due. They would have known that from his sister. She would have told them that her puritanical brother was coming in from Ohio and she didn't want any procurers around while he was in town. Any deal they had in mind to make with you and Milton could wait. If necessary they could even go out to River Forks and pick that bit of business up again. But here was Mr. Jellicoe and he was more immediate. He was a valued client. He would be good for a lot of future business. He would be in the market for a replacement for the late Sydney Bell and more immediately he was always profitably grateful when they rescued him from driving when drunk. More than that, he was in that shop buying a dangerous souvenir. They

232

could protect him from involving himself with the Sydney Bell killing and when he came to his senses he would be all the more grateful and, therefore, all the more profitable. They left you for Mr. Jellicoe, and since we were also interested in Sydney Bell's sinful clothes, we were right outside the shop in time to see them pick Mr. Jellicoe up."

Up to this point Jellicoe, to all appearances, had been completely concentrated on Bannerman. He never wilted under the man's baleful gaze. He sat there looking at Bannerman in mingled sympathy and bewilderment. As I read him, here was that good kid's brother and now the good kid was dead. He was sorry for her brother. He would have been more than ready to grieve with him, but the brother wasn't grieving. Instead he was calling that good kid unpleasant names, and that was something K. R. E. Jellicoe just couldn't begin to understand. I would have guessed that he was hardly listening to this story Gibby was building up with the girl, but he must have had some attention for it because he did rise to the bit about his buying the dangerous souvenir.

"It looked just like hers," he said. "If it wasn't hers it was one just like it. You know I was a little drunk anyhow and I never even thought that maybe it wasn't hers. I wanted it."

"And your friends didn't want you to have it," Gibby said. "They had to beat the daylights out of you to get it away from you and they did get it, all but a small piece of the lace."

Jellicoe shook his head. "It wasn't George and Harry gave me this," he said, touching lightly the square of gauze that was fixed to his face with the Scotch tape. "That was something else I got into later when I was

233

even drunker. They just tried to take the nightgown away from me and I was hanging on to it and it tore and I was left with just the piece of it." With every word he was looking more and more pouty. "I haven't even got that now," he said sadly. "I got mad at George and Harry and I went off on my own. I got a lot drunker and I got in this fight somewhere where I did get beat up. Not that it's anything. The thing that burns me I was rolled or something. I haven't even got the piece of lace any more."

"You had a bad night," Gibby said sympathetically.

"Some nights, they're like that." Jellicoe gave it the philosophically resigned touch.

Gibby returned to Joan Loomis. He went through all the lying she had done, all that business about phoning Ellie's apartment and getting no answer, her little device about the wrong number. The girl denied nothing. She had done all that Gibby was charging against her, but she had done it for Milton. It may have been foolish, she conceded, but she insisted that it hadn't been wrong. Milton, she said, was good, and it was Milton's goodness that had made everything right. The one point she did labor was Milton's innocence. He hadn't killed his sister. He hadn't killed anyone. Only in that had she been really wrong, in thinking even for a moment that he might have killed Ellie. Now she had only one regret and that was that she had failed in her efforts to keep from him the knowledge of what his sister had been.

She told us about going to the station to meet Bannerman's train. While waiting, she had spotted one of the men who had been following her around for so much of the day, but she'd had no thought beyond the assumption that this was a masher and that it was bad luck that she had run into him again. Gibby did question that a bit. He wondered at her being all that ready to accept a coincidence of this sort in a city like New York with all its millions of men. They kicked it around for a while and Gibby was satisfied. Joan Loomis had learned her bitter lessons on the subject of how different New York was from River Forks but this was a difference that hadn't been in the area of her learning. At home one was always running into the same people all over town. She should have known that it wouldn't be like that here, but she had just not thought of it.

"But even on the assumption that the man was only a masher," Gibby said, "he did make you nervous. When Milton came up behind you and covered your eyes, you didn't hesitate for a moment. You were certain that it would be this man who had been following you all over town. You whirled around and let him have it."

"What else was I to think? Milton's train hadn't come in yet. There was no one I knew in New York."

"Exactly," Gibby said. "And what followed was just as automatic. You saw that it wasn't the man who had been following you. It was Milton—and Milton's train hadn't come in yet. The very thing you had been trying all day not to believe was right there before your eyes. Milton had come earlier than expected. He had gone to Ellie's apartment and had caught her in the act or so soon after the act that he couldn't possibly be deceived. The shock of it had knocked him over. He had fastened his hands around her throat and had choked the life out of her. He had killed her with those very hands which a moment before he had playfully put over your eyes. You fainted. What else would a girl do at a moment like that?"

"All right," Joan said defiantly. "I've told you this before. I did think it. I was wrong, but I did think it. I wasn't making sense. I see that now, but all I could think of was that Milton had killed her and that he had had every right to kill her and that the only thing that was wrong about it would be that he would have to suffer for it. That's what gave me the courage to sit with you for hours and lie and lie and lie. I never lied before in my life and I never thought I could make myself be a liar, but I could and I did and I'll never be ashamed of it. Mistaken as I was, it wasn't wrong."

Gibby grinned at her. "It wasn't particularly good either," he said. "It didn't convince me or Mac but we're old hands with liars. It wouldn't have had to be especially good to convince Milton, who'd led a sheltered life, but it wasn't even that good. He started distrusting you. When you went back to your hotel, he went down to the lobby and hung around watching. He saw you go out and he followed you."

"I know. I went out to see if I could find the man. You had taken my fingerprints and I had never thought of fingerprints. I knew you were going to find out all about me, everything I'd done in Ellie's apartment. I went a little crazy, I suppose. I know I was thinking six ways at once. I couldn't talk to Milton about it because I couldn't even begin without telling him what Ellie was really like. There was this man who had been following me. You showed a lot of interest in this man and I began to wonder whether he was only what I had been thinking. I was wondering if he couldn't have been someone who knew something about Ellie. I had to find him. I had to talk to him. I was desperate. I had to know more if I was going to help Milton. I could see that what I'd already done wouldn't help at all. It was going to be no good because of the fingerprints. I had to find the man. Even if he had been just following me, even if he didn't know anything about Ellie or about anything, I had to find him. You see, I was even thinking that if he knew nothing, I could still do something to help Milton. I could go with the man and then you would think I was the kind of girl that did those things and, since you would know about me from the fingerprints anyhow, you'd think I killed Ellie. I could help Milton that way."

Bannerman's eyes had turned away from Jellicoe. He was looking at the girl now and all the anger and hate were gone. Horror had taken their place.

"What made you think the man would still be in the station?" Gibby asked.

"That was where I had last seen him. I didn't know any other place to look. He was still there and I went to him and spoke to him. At first he acted as though he knew nothing. He said he'd been watching me, trying to remember where he had met me before."

"Treated it like an ordinary pickup?" Gibby asked.

She couldn't quite answer that. She had never been involved in a pickup before and she had no idea of how they went. She did describe the exchanges between George and herself, however, and it was obvious that he had handled it as an ordinary pickup. He had invited her to go and have a drink with him. He had taken her as far as the house where all the police had been. It was evident that that had been Harry's place. We probably had narrowly missed running into them there. Then he had said that he had forgotten that the place they were going to had moved but there was a good enough place back down the street. He had taken her to the bar.

In the bar he had excused himself for a few minutes and when he had returned, he had said something about thinking he remembered where they had met.

"At Sydney Bell's place?" Gibby asked.

"Yes."

"Had you met this man before?"

"No. I met none of her friends. She would just talk to people on the telephone, but she didn't have me meet anyone."

"I see," Gibby said. "So then he went on and fed you another bit and another bit, narrowing down until he had hinted pretty strongly that he was thinking of Sydney Bell's apartment early that morning when you had been up there rearranging the dead girl's life for her."

Joan nodded. "Yes," she said. "He told me I was in trouble, terrible trouble, but I wasn't to worry. He was going to help me. He said he had influence. He knew people. He said there wasn't anything that couldn't be fixed if you knew the right people. He asked me a lot of questions about Milton and he kept saying I could tell him everything. He was my friend and he was going to help us, Milton and me. He knew the right people."

"Then Miss Sylvester came and joined you," Gibby said. "Did he say she was the right people?"

"He said she was a friend of Ellie's, except that he called Ellie Sydney and Miss Sylvester called her that, too. He left the table again and went to the back. Miss Sylvester said she hated bars. She said she hated them particularly when she didn't have a man with her. Two women alone in a bar, it would be only a matter of time before some drunk would be getting fresh. She said we could go to her place. We could talk better there."

"What about the guy who brought you?" Gibby asked. "Didn't you think you should have waited for him?"

"He was gone so long and when I said we ought to wait for him, she said he would come around to her place. He had gone away for a while. There had been something he had to do. She said it was something he had to do for me. I asked her what, but she said I wasn't to worry. They were taking care of everything."

"What made you trust these people?" Gibby asked. "You hadn't met any of them before. They were strangers, or so you say."

"They were strangers, but they had been Ellie's friends. There were all sorts of things they told me about Milt and myself that they couldn't possibly have known unless Ellie had been their friend and had told them about us. It wasn't that I really trusted them. I was desperate and I was terribly, terribly mistaken. I had no choice, I thought. Things were so bad and I hadn't the first idea of how soon it would be that you would know about me because of the fingerprints. They said you'd been lying to me when you said you wanted my prints only for identification because I'd been staying there with Ellie. They said you could tell from where you'd find the prints just which ones were from my having stayed there and which showed what I had been doing there after Ellie was killed. I was grasping at straws. Things were so bad that I couldn't see how they could be any worse."

"So you went with her?"

The rest of it was as we had already had it from Bannerman. She had gone with Mabel Sylvester to this fine house in the East Fifties. The woman had let them in with her key. There had been no one about, no servants or anyone else. Miss Sylvester had talked to her and urged her to tell everything. The line had been that they had to know everything she had done and everything Milton had done if they were going to be of any help.

She had only talked a little before they were interrupted by the ringing of the doorbell. Miss Sylvester had gone down to open the door. It had been Milton and he had demanded to see Joan. Miss Sylvester had asked him in. After that she had talked to the two of them.

"That was when Milton found out," the girl said.

It must have been quite a scene. The Sylvester woman told him flatly that it was no good lying to her. She knew that he had killed his sister. He had denied it hotly. He loved his sister. He had been both mother and father to her. He had been more than a brother. Miss Sylvester had laughed in his face. She had told him straight out what his precious Ellie had been doing, and at that point Milton had blown his top.

"At first he wouldn't believe her," Joan Loomis moaned. "Then he began saying all those things he's been saying to you. He said he would have killed Ellie himself if he had known and she pounced on it and said that he had killed Ellie. She knew all about it. Heaven forgive me. I believed her."

It had been at that point that Milton Bannerman had washed his hands of everything, including in everything his sister's memory. He was ready to take Joan out of there and go straight back home to River Forks with her. Mabel Sylvester had stopped him in his tracks. She'd told him what choices he had. He could let her help him,

240

and maybe she could fix everything. He could go to the police and confess or he could do as he said he was going to do and see Joan arrested for his sister's murder. She told him what Joan had done in Ellie's apartment.

"She told him how you were going to know because of my fingerprints," Joan said, and now the girl was white and shaking.

It wasn't only that scene that she was finding so hard to describe. It was more what she next had to tell us. There had been a second interruption, again the doorbell. They had been in an upstairs sitting room and Mabel Sylvester had left them up there while she went down to answer the bell. She hadn't returned. They had waited and waited and then they had gone downstairs to look for her. They had found her. It was the same story as we had already had from Milton Bannerman except that Joan wasn't pretending that they had only just discovered the body at the time when we had arrived. There had been some time in between. She didn't know just how long because she had been terrified and minutes could have seemed like hours.

They had taken out their handkerchiefs and had begun wiping. They had wiped the railings of the stairs and the doorknobs of the upstairs room. They had gone about that room, wiping everything. They'd had no memory of what they had touched and what they hadn't, but they had wiped everything just to be certain.

"You were profiting by your mistake in Ellie's apartment," Gibby said.

"I couldn't even think," the girl answered. "I was sick with fear and horror and I was happy, too, because then I knew. I knew how mistaken I had been. It hadn't been Milton at all because Milton was upstairs with me all the time. She went down to answer the bell and we waited for her and when we went down we went down together and she looked just like Ellie had looked, so it couldn't have been Milton. He said we had to wipe everything clean and I did what he said. I was through with thinking. I had been such a complete fool."

"Yes," Gibby said. "Milton was smarter. He knew about fingerprints. You may not know it but the reason why we had it so easy spotting your fingerprints in the apartment was because before you went around the place touching things yesterday morning, the slate had been wiped clean. Everything had been wiped before you got there, just the kind of job Milton had you do with him here after Mabel Sylvester had been killed. Even in that respect this killing is a duplicate of his sister's murder."

"But he was upstairs with me," Joan screamed. She saw the closing trap and she was trying to claw her way out of it.

"We have only your word for it," Gibby said. "Do you think that's going to be enough? After all, it's only the word of a girl who thinks anything goes so long as she can save pure, unsullied Milton Bannerman."

"You must believe me," the girl said.

"Who's going to make a jury believe you?" Gibby asked. "The wages of sin are death and, boy, has this been pay day! Ellie, the sinner, was killed in her bed and she hadn't been looking at television when she died. The set had been turned on twenty-four hours before you came down from Boston and it had been turned on to screen any noise that might have been made while the place was being wiped clean of all prints. But Ellie was only the beginning. Ellie had really been something when she was alive. She had been the girl who kept knocking them dead. Look at Mr. Jellicoe here with his bit of red lace to remember her by. So the sinner was killed, but that wasn't enough. There were the men who led her into sin. There was Harry and he got it just as he came out of his shower. He never even got the soap out of his eyes before the strangler's hands closed around his throat. You can't alibi Milton for that one. You were on your own then with a man you picked up in the station. Then you were in the bar with that man and Milton was outside and Mabel Sylvester came along in her car. She parked it not out front but down the alley. She parked it there for George because that wasn't a healthy street for him, not with so many police around. George had telephoned her to tell her that the police were clustered around Harry's place and that he had you in the bar down the street. He didn't know that Milton was lying in wait outside the bar."

"He wasn't lying in wait," Joan protested. "He was following us, worrying about me."

"His story and your story. A jury will have to choose between that story and this one I'm telling you. Milton was lying in wait outside. His sinful sister had come to her just deserts. One of her procurers had come to his just down the street. Now Milton was watching the other procurer and Mabel Sylvester had the good sense to be worried. She was worried about George because it looked very much as though something had happened to Harry and what had happened to Harry could happen to George. She may not have known whether it was murder or merely a Vice Squad raid, but she would worry about either. If it was murder again, then she had further worries. There was Mr. Jellicoe, their best client. Wasn't he in danger? Wasn't she in danger herself? She was a brave woman. She told George to get out of town. She told him she would come around in her car and leave it in the alley for him. She told him to take the car and get out of town, go up to Westport and stay with Jellicoe. He would be safe there from New York's Vice Squad if it was that and if it was the other, pay day for the wages of sin, he could watch over Jellicoe and Jellicoe could watch over him. Meanwhile she would see what she could find out from this girl."

I was way ahead of the story at this point because, after all, I had been up in Westport with Gibby. I had been there when the rock had smashed against his head. I could still feel the strangler's fingers on my throat. George had been in the bar. Milton had been waiting outside. On his own admission he had seen Mabel Sylvester come out of the alley. George had taken the car and driven to Westport but he hadn't known that he had a passenger crouched down in back. He hadn't known it till they had reached the Jellicoe place and the fingers had closed around his throat. The rest followed simply enough. George had died. The Westport cop, of course, had been only incidental. The killer's work had still to be finished and we'd come along at a time when we might have stopped him with the last of his work undone. He took the red sedan from Jellicoe's garage, drove back to New York, parked it at the end of the subway line, took the subway downtown, and killed the procuress.

Gibby turned to Jellicoe. "That leaves only you," he said.

"Gee," Jellicoe muttered. "Why me?"

"You're the man who corrupted Ellie Bannerman," Gibby said.

"That's a lie. We had our parties. I'm not denying it, but I wasn't the first. I've only known her for a month or a little more. She had been there before."

"I don't doubt it," Gibby said. "But when it's pay day, there aren't these fine distinctions. The man who first corrupted Ellie Bannerman came and went years ago. That must have been some time shortly after she came to New York, but you did enjoy her favors. Look at her brother. He's ready to kill you. In his mind adultery is adultery and there are no distinctions."

"Just because the kid was enjoying her life?" Jellicoe bleated.

"It's all a matter of what your standards are," Gibby told him. "You think nothing is as important as enjoying yourself. He thinks nothing is as important as righteousness and virtue. He would kill his sister because she hadn't refused her favors. You would kill her because she had refused them."

"She was a good kid," Jellicoe muttered. "She was more fun than a parcel of monkeys."

"We know she never refused you," Gibby continued. "It's a great pity that you had been drinking with her and you couldn't understand when she told you that you were going to have to stay away because her brother was coming to town. You didn't mean to hurt her, but you didn't understand what she was saying and you started choking her and you choked her too much."

"You just said he killed her," Jellicoe shouted. "He killed all the others. You just been showing how he did it."

"I've been showing how he could have done it. You

245

killed Sydney Bell and then you went running in a
panic to your friends—Mae and George and Harry.
They were going to fix it for you. They knew how. They
could fix anything for a price. They asked you if after
the killing you had thought to wipe away fingerprints.
You hadn't, of course. They went to the apartment and
they wiped it clean. They did all the careful things you
didn't have the brains to do for yourself. They even
clipped her fingernails right down to the quick and beyond so that we couldn't find any scrapings under them
since they would be scrapings of you. They didn't tell
you anything or ask you to do any part of it. You were
just to leave it to them and do as they told you and you
were to pay."

"Look," Jellicoe protested. "Just because I laid her.
That's all I ever did. I laid her."

"It started that way. Then you killed her and they
were taking care of it. But they knew you. You were a
sentimental slob and they weren't taking any chances
on your doing something silly that would give it all
away. They watched you and they watched the apartment. George was watching the apartment when Miss
Loomis got there. He thought that would bring the police and when it didn't, they knew she could be worth
watching as well. The time could come when it might
be possible to put it on her or at least to make some
profitable use of her and of the silly things she was
doing to screen Bannerman. Then you were just as silly
as they'd expected you'd be. You bought the nightgown.
They took you in tow and they got you to a quiet
place where the two of them could work you over and
get it away from you. That wasn't a fight. It was a beat-
ing. They were teaching you that you would not only

have to pay but that you would have to stay in line as well. You got away from them then, but it wasn't enough. Staying in line wasn't going to be any fun and what is life if there isn't fun in it? Meanwhile you had learned something or you thought you had. You thought you could kill and get away with it. All you had to do was remember to wear gloves for it or wipe off fingerprints if you couldn't manage gloves. You didn't know there could be a million other things you'd have to watch. You were never going to have any fun again or any freedom ever as long as George and Mae and Harry were alive. You started after them. First you went to Harry's and got him. Then you went after Mae. You were the passenger crouched down in the back of Mae's car when she drove around to the bar. You were waiting for a chance to get at her but you couldn't while she was driving busy streets. Then George took the car over. He didn't drive busy streets. He drove up to Westport because they had to find you before you did any other silly things. Something had happened to Harry and whatever it was, it was dangerous, and they had to find you. You saw where he was heading and you let him take you all the way. He was taking you to just the spot you would have chosen for yourself. You killed George. You were making certain he was dead when we came along. We were in your way and you went after us. You got the cop but you fumbled me and you fumbled Mac. You smashed the lock on your own garage door and you took your own red sedan and drove back to New York. Then you came down here and you finished the job. You got Mae. You thought you were being clever coming around here to look for your car. You weren't clever enough."

"Look," Jellicoe argued. "I'm not smart. Anybody can tell you I'm not smart. I'm not smart enough to do any of this stuff. I can't even understand it when you're telling it. Him, now. He's smart and it's like you said. He's got a reason."

"Brother, you aren't smart," Gibby told him. "You aren't even as smart as you think you are. You weren't smart enough to clip Harry's fingernails close not even after he'd tried for your face after your doctor had changed the fastenings on your dressings to Scotch tape because he thought adhesive tape wasn't becoming. You weren't smart enough to think that Scotch tape will chip off and cling under a man's nails. We found a bit under Harry's. You see, you needed them to clean up after you. You were no good at cleaning up after yourself. You did it again up in Westport. You smashed the lock on your garage but the wood isn't splintered inward or outward as it would have to be if you had forced the door. You did it the easy way. You opened the door with your key and you took a rock to the lock and smashed it then. You smashed downward on it. The wood is splintered in that direction and it couldn't be unless the door was opened before the lock was smashed. You weren't smart enough to know how to get rid of your blood-spattered clothes after you killed that cop and half killed Mac and me. You went up to the house and changed into completely fresh clothes and you took the stuff you'd been wearing—it was all brown and yellow to match your convertible and I suppose you don't have a red and chromium suit to match the sedan—you took it outside and set fire to it. You weren't smart enough to know that clothes are hard to burn. There will be scraps left with blood on them. Just because they made such a smoky fire, you thought they were burning fine. We would have found them long ago if it hadn't been that you had half killed us, and when we came to and were coughing like crazy with the smoke, we were still too muzzy to wonder what was burning to make all that smoke."

That was as far as Gibby got and then things went crazy. Cops or no cops, Bannerman did charge out of his chair and go for Jellicoe. The cops grabbed Bannerman and he dragged them with him. They were so busy with him that they didn't even notice that Jellicoe was breaking for the door, or possibly they just thought he was afraid of Bannerman. Anyhow it fell to Gibby and me to bring him down. I came out of it all right, but a couple of the stitches in Gibby's ear pulled open. He was bleeding again when he had to answer to Milton Bannerman and the girl. They wanted to know why he had frightened them by building the whole case against Milton when he had known even before we had ever come to Mabel Sylvester's house that Jellicoe was our man.

"I was teaching you what it meant to fool around with murder," Gibby said.

It was enough answer for them since they were who they were and they had such a strong belief in being punished for their transgressions. I knew Gibby better than that. I could look back over the whole session and see how he had built it to get out of them every last shred of their story, however soiled and however sordid. He needed that story to fill out the chinks in the case against Jellicoe and he had done the job.